This story touched me in many ways. Having lost two brothers myself, I identified with the heartache of Josiah and Senora at the unexpected loss of their brother. Lorie makes the wisdom of the Bible come alive as Senora and Josiah go on a wild and dangerous journey to find each other and find healing.

Stacey Greene
--Author of *Letters to the Dead Men* and *Stronger Than Broken*
www.StaceyGreeneCoachng.com

"From the opening words of her novel, Lorie Gurnett speaks directly to her readers on issues they face daily. Her book is not only a positive and uplifting story for young adults, but it also invites them into a magical world full of color, light, and empowerment. Her narrative is especially empowering for young girls who have been bullied, who suffer from depression, and who experience more grief than some adults. She writes about the hard topics pre-teens and teenagers face without glorifying it. Instead, she gives young readers powerful tools to help them fight through their adolescence with confidence and faith."

Tina Morlock
--Editor and published author

What a great story! Lorie Gurnett has written a must read for anyone who may be struggling. Full of interesting characters and an exciting fantasy world! This book will remind readers that with faith, courage, and the bond of family anything is possible!

Stacey Armstrong

We all need a place we can retreat away from our day to day, to be recharged, encouraged, and even entertained. What better way than a read of Lorie Gurnett's first fantasy novel as she mixes fantasy with the value of Christian faith and family. Enjoy!!!

Dallas Block
--Executive Director
https://rocksolidrefuge.com/

Lorie Gurnett has a way of challenging her readers to explore and discover their true identity. Through the art of storytelling Lorie helps her readers understand that though they may face many struggles, they do not face them alone. Moreover, God will not waste our pain, but will redeem all things; therefore, hope is always victorious and shines brighter than our darkest day and our hardest nights. This is a story worth reading.

Joan Turley
--Award Nominated Author of Sacred Work in Secular Places

What a beautiful and compelling story about two siblings that embark into an adventure to uncover a "treasure". It's a thrilling fantasy book full of magic, mystery and twists, but at the end, there is a powerful message. Message of hope, faith, family bonds and friendship. A must read for everyone!

Liliana Moir

I really enjoyed the book. I felt like I was journeying with the characters and wondering what was around the next bend in the road. There is lots of adventure and interesting characters. The themes of family and redemption were very beautiful. I am excited to share this book with my children; I think they will love it!

Andrea Carlson

Lorie Gurnett challenges her readers to look at who they are and reminds them that though they may face obstacles, they do not face them alone. She reassures her readers that they are important, they have a purpose, and there is hope no matter what darkness they may face.

April Gurnett

Lorie's novel shows both the beauty and pain that can occur within families. It also shows how the love of God can make a wonderful difference. Lovely read.

Aislinn Bell

Treasure Kingdom

To: Andrea,

Thank you for believing in me. You are stronger than you think. Never give up.

Treasure Kingdom

LORIE GURNETT

FOREWORD BY:
JOHN SCHLITT, LEAD SINGER OF PETRA

Published by Author Academy Elite
PO Box 43, Powell, OH 43035
www.AuthorAcademyElite.com

LCCN: 2019905829
ISBN: 978-1-64085-670-7 (Paperback)
ISBN: 978-1-64085-671-4 (Hardcover)
ISBN: 978-1-64085-670-7 (Ebook)

Available in paperback, hardback, e-book, and audiobook

All Scripture quotations, unless otherwise indicated, are taken from the Holy Bible, New International Version®, ESV®. Copyright © 1973, 1978, 1984 by Biblica, Inc.TM. All rights reserved worldwide.

Book Cover Designed by: PhoenixDesigns23 from 99design.

In loving memory of my daddy,
William E. Moir,
who taught me to pursue my dreams,
push through the hard times,
and find my strength in living my hearts desires.
(Sept. 28, 1941- May 20, 2018)

To my loving father in-law Richard G. Gurnett,
who taught me to put my heart and soul into
everything I do, to get back up when I get knocked down,
and to trust God for everything else
for He is the one who holds both my heart
and my future.
(Feb. 26, 1946- Feb. 28, 2018)

Thank you to my loving and supportive husband,
Mervyn R. Gurnett. You taught me
to never give up, that hope will hold us together,
and to always lean on God for clarity and guidance.
you are the strongest person I know;
thank you for believing in me.

And a final thank you for my children---
Logan L. Gurnett and Aurora N. L. Gurnett.
Logan, you have taught me that through
strength and determination all things are possible.
Aurora, you have taught me to believe in myself,
to trust in God's direction, and
that my hope is found in my identity in Christ my Saviour.

I could not have accomplished this without all of you.

Table of Content

Part 1, The Fight

Part 2, The Voice Of Fear

Part 3, The Risk Is Real

Part 4, Doubts Of Fear

Part 5, From Confusion To Clarity

Foreword

By: John Schlitt
Lead Singer of Petra

I have travelled all over the world singing and speaking, connecting with believers in many different countries. It's as if we are family, even though I've never met most of the people that attend my concerts. I have seen and experienced the growth of the Christian faith in places you would never think possible. The world says that the Christian faith is getting smaller, that the number of Christians throughout the world is shrinking. But in reality, Christianity remains the largest religious group. People are looking for answers – and finding them in Jesus Christ. It took me a long time to realize that; it wasn't until I was 30 years old that I figured it out.

I started out singing as a kid and it grew from there. I almost flunked out of college because of music; it's hard to pass your classes when you're up until all hours of the night playing a gig. So I had to quit music in order to finish school. My parents were very good people and all they asked is that I get a college degree, which I did. After graduating with a civil engineering degree, I went right back into music.

For eight years I was in Head East, a secular band that hit the big time. I was living the musician's dream, playing to massive crowds at major venues as the headlining act and touring with bands such as Journey, Van Halen, Boston, Heart, Kansas and many others in the '70s. After a while, this became commonplace – and boring. You may have an amazing dream, but when you live it night after night, it's not so special any more. I needed another thrill. I was introduced to cocaine... and I was hooked.

For the next two years, cocaine ruled my life. Everything else, including my family, was a distant second. It all came to a distressing end in 1980 when I was let go by the band. The reason: I had an out-of-control drug and alcohol addiction. My whole life was the band. It came before my family, before my health - before anything. And all of a sudden it's gone. So for the next six months I go on this binge; cocaine to get high, alcohol to come down... I was either high or drunk 24 hours a day. I'm building a new band, I told everyone, and I had to be on top of my game. The truth is, I was just in a haze and it was a great excuse to stay high.

During this same six month period that I'm going on this binge, my wife comes to know Christ - but I didn't want to hear anything about it. I didn't need this Jesus stuff; I figured I'd become a Christian when I'm rich, famous, and too old to do anything else.

Then, the morning after our wedding anniversary, I woke up on the couch. The night before I had been on a drinking binge and couldn't get any cocaine to bring me back up to go to our anniversary party. So my wife just let me pass out on the couch and she went by herself. I woke up to my two year old son staring at me with a look on his face that said "Who are you?" It broke my heart...

At that moment I heard a voice say, "John, you are worth more dead than alive." I totally agreed, and started planning my demise.

But the Enemy keeps forgetting that we have a God who loves us so much; He knows the plan. Satan doesn't fool Him! Satan doesn't have free rein to do what he wants. He may talk a big talk, but God is there saying, "Nope. You're not gonna get away with this!"

In Treasure Kingdom, in darkness and pain because of not knowing who she is, Senora questions if life is worth living. After tragically losing her oldest brother Trevor, she could find no hope or joy.

I too had no hope or joy left. It was time to leave this world and let me wife get on with her life - without me. I had decided I wasn't going to use a gun because I didn't want my kids to see the mess. So I sat there figuring out what kind of pills I could use that would be quick and painless as possible. As I contemplated how I was going to end my life, my wife tapped me on the shoulder and said, "Now remember John, you promised you would come and talk to my pastor." I asked her when I had said that. She replied, "last night when you were drunk." OK, fine. Can't argue with that.

As you read this book, you will discover that God has a plan for your life and will give you the determination and tools to stand firm against adversity, and bring others alongside you to help.

I went to the pastor's house with a mindset that it was not going to change a thing. I agreed to go so that after I was gone, my wife could say "he tried." I had already made my plan and nothing was going to stop me. But I didn't realize that within that house was the Holy Spirit – and He was not going to let me walk out the door without Him. I got hit with boldness about Jesus that I've never known before… I was brought to Christ that night and it was a new beginning for me.

I went in with an attitude and I walked out with the Lord; He has walked with me ever since.

It fascinates me that people can choose to face the world's problems without Him. Christ wants to offer you everything, and people shake their heads and say, "I don't want that everything stuff." They choose to suffer. They have been blinded by the world. Robert shows this attitude since he also feels he is not worth saving and blames himself for Trevor's death.

When we try to tell others about our faith or invite them to church, we should not be surprised when they say no. The world is constantly telling us that we don't know who we are or what power we have behind us. You will discover how worthy you are as you follow Josiah and Senora through this journey of discovery. What is the greatest treasure? How do they find their self worth and the strength to become an immovable force?

The Enemy doesn't want to let you go. When you follow Christ, the temptations are more than ever before. Satan doesn't want to lose! I fell multiple times, but I had people who loved me, cared for me, brought me in, cleaned the wounds, and prayed for me.

In the past, I had used coke to get up, booze to come back down, and in the middle was the perfect spot. I have since learned that that perfect spot was sobriety! What God wanted to give me for free, what He wanted to bless me with - the Enemy was charging me big bucks for. It's terrible how Satan plays games with us all day long. I was convinced that God couldn't use me because of my past. I thought I knew God's plan, and in my mind – it did not include music. Just as Senora and Josiah discovered that God can use them even in their own mess - God can use us too.

For five years I assumed I'd never sing again, because I'd blown it with so much garbage. Singing was in the past for me – and that was fine, because I knew God had a plan and

I was anxious to see what it was. By now it was a cost and scheduling engineer – I finally put that college degree to work.

One day, as I was contemplating my life without music - because of my own doing, a thought came to me: exactly what sin had I done that was greater than the blood of Christ? Remember, there is not one sin that we can commit that is greater than the sacrifice that Jesus made on the cross. This is when I began to realize that maybe God could still use me despite my past.

Bob Hartman, one of the founders of the Christian rock band Petra, a band I was a big fan of, contacted me about becoming their lead singer. When Bob called me I thought someone was playing a joke! But my wife and I knew... we knew this was God at work. I was getting a second chance.

Since then I've sung on more than 25 albums, on television programs, special events and concerts throughout the world. All this from someone who thought they would never sing again!

God is a God of second chances... no matter how bad you blow it or how bad your past may be – God can take your life and turn it around for His good purpose. I'm living proof of that – and if He can change my life - He can certainly do the same for you!

Preface

We all face dark moments in our lives. Many times we struggle with who we are and what our purpose in life is. This book is a reminder that no matter how dark life seems, we are never alone and we have strength within us. God loves you very much and He believes in you. Never lose hope, for darkness is forced to flee from the light. Never give up, you are stronger then you think.

Acknowledgments

I would like to thank my loving husband, Merv, and my two children, Logan and Aurora for all of the support and encouragement I have received from them. They always encouraged me to never give up and to continue writing. Thank you to all my beta readers and those who helped edit this book: Donna Porrett, Gwen Mathieu, Cordie Moir, Stacey Green, Sandra Fram, Tina Morlock, Stacey Armstrong, Andrea Carlson, Aislinn Bell, April Gurnett, Liliana Moir, and Tannis Bissett. Thank you for your endorsements Joan Turley and Dallas Block. I would like to send a huge thank you to John Schlitt for writing my foreword, it is an honour. Thank you to Author Academy Elite, for believing in me. Thank you Kary Oberbrunner for always reminding me there is always support and hope, no matter what I face. Thank you Daphne Smith for accepting me into AAE, and for your many encouraging words.

PART 1

The Fight

THE JOURNEY BEGINS

Your words and actions determine who you are.

Are you guarding your tongue?

CHAPTER 1

The Journey Begins

A gun fires from a distance. The stench of blood lingers in her nostrils, and the sounds of sirens and squealing tires are a painful reminder of what happened that day. It haunts her every time she closes her eyes. She recalls how the phone clanged as it slipped out of her mom's hands when she received the call from Bobbie's mom. Fear boiled deep within as they rushed to the scene. The sight of her oldest brother, Trevor, lying lifeless on the floor almost overwhelmed her. Bobbie, Trevor's best friend leaned over him, as he tried to breathe life back; while the blood pooled around his lifeless body. Emergency responders pulled Bobbie away to inspect the situation. Bobbie's mom spoke in riddles and barked out orders at him. There was yelling, finger pointing, and mom was trying to make sense of what Bobbie's mom was telling her. Senora's anger and fear clawed at her and screamed to get out. She screamed at Bobbie, "How could you let this happen? I thought you cared about Trevor. I guess I was wrong."

Her dad didn't even take time off work to come home for Trevor's funeral. "What will it take for dad to come home? Does he not care about any of us anymore?" She whispers under her breath as she tried to make sense of everything that had happened. It was only six months ago, but it's still fresh in her mind like it happened yesterday. Age 21 was far too young for Trevor's life to be over already.

She stands and makes her way down the stairs. The old grandfather clock chimes two a.m. as she passes it on her way to the kitchen. A family photo hanging on the wall stops her in her tracks. She stares at it with both sadness and joy. She sees herself sleeping on top of her dad's shoulders, her mom resting her elbow on Trevor's shoulders and Josiah hanging on a nearby tree. They all look so happy. "I miss those yearly camping trips. Life seemed so simple back then. I miss you so much, Trevor," she whispers as she continues towards the kitchen. Tonight, the darkness seems heavy and pushes in on her from all directions. A flood of memories hits her with full force.

At school, kids push her away, and when she tries to join in a conversation, she finds herself being the center of their jokes and threats. She remembers when Trevor used to help her prepare for her science projects, but now when she tries to ask Josiah, he makes fun of her and questions her—why isn't she smart enough to figure things out on her own? The other day, she decided to go for a walk to clear her head and try to find something to smile about when she got knocked to the ground from behind. When she turned to see who it was, Bobbie, or as she calls him now, Robert, smiles sheepishly back at her. "Nora, I haven't seen you all summer. Where have you been?"

"You know, around. There's nowhere else to go." Senora rolls her eyes sarcastically.

"I hear ya there. Where has Jo been hiding lately?"

"Where else? Camp. He comes back in a few days. Why did you knock me down?" Senora glares.

"Oh, did I knock you down? I was just trying to get your attention. Anyways, say hi to Jo for me. I'll be seeing ya in school soon." He turns and rides his bike away.

Senora shudders at the thought that summer is ending and soon she will have to face another year of torture and threats. Plus, this year she has to deal with it without Trevor. Senora remembers how she used to joke around with Trevor, and he would encourage Senora to be a better person. He had such kind words and wanted to help others in need. Now, Senora is so angry and holds everyone at arm's length.

No matter what she says or does, she feels like she will mess everything up. Why does everything have to be so hard? Why does everyone seem to be against her? Wave upon wave of colliding questions, so many unanswered. All her life she has been bombarded with messages that tell her she shouldn't try because she will never amount to anything. Messages that say—she's too skinny, too fat, she needs to eat more, needs to talk less. These messages of discouragement and sorrow leave her feeling lost and confused.

When Senora was 14, her dad dove into his work. He said that the more sales he makes more money he brings in. Senora never understood why he had to travel so far for sell pens and advertising. The marketing business was always confusing to her. She was daddy's little girl, but he isn't around much now, leaving her feeling abandoned. She only wanted her dad to hold her and tell her that everything would be fine, but he was never home.

When a young man showed an interest and told her she was beautiful, even though she was not supposed to date, she did anyway. She only wanted someone to see her and to love her. It was the biggest mistake of her life. It ended badly and left her feeling worthless.

Senora's sadness was growing; the pain in her heart was starting to weigh her down. The words that she will never amount to anything, that she messes everything up, and that she is not worth even to be loved cut through her, and she felt boxed in. Maybe the kids at school were right. She thought to herself, *why am I here? I feel like I bring misery to everyone around me.* Why shouldn't she be made to feel worse? She wanted to hide in her room, find the smallest corner in her closet, and to vanish away. She saw a knife on the counter, and nobody else was around. *Nobody would miss her, everyone would be better off without her,* she thinks. "Nobody likes me; everybody hates me. I think I'll go eat worms." The words dance around in her mind, screaming at her.

But when flashes of good memories start to flood her thoughts: camping trips and dad playing bucking bronco and trying to knock the kids off his back. Josiah always seemed to win when they played, but Trevor helped her throughout whatever game they played. Tonight, she remembers Trevor joking around, as she followed him and laughed while they raced up a hill. "Hurry up you two, you'll miss it!" Trevor laughed excitedly as he ran up the hill. Senora, being the youngest, was only eight at the time. She pushed herself hard to keep up with her 10-year-old-brother, Josiah, but Trevor being 15, was always the fastest.

"Hurry up, Nora, Trevor's surprises never disappoint." Josiah laughed. When they reached the top of the hill, the sun illuminated the sky. The ocean looked as if it was on fire, mirroring the sky in all its beauty.

"Nora, Jo. You made it," Trevor says.

"Would have made it sooner, if she'd hurried up," Josiah says under his breath.

"Now, now, Jo. Be nice. Let's just enjoy the view. The ocean always brings me peace. Nora, these are the times to remember." Trevor's words echo in her ears as Senora slowly opens her eyes.

A small smile formed on her face, and she chuckled at the memories. She felt if she could still laugh at a single memory, then maybe there was hope somewhere. The knife slips from her fingertips and crashes to the floor. She quickly picks it up and cautiously looks around, hoping no one heard her. She quietly puts the knife back in the block and pours herself a glass of water. Senora was not sure where or if she would be able to find meaning in her life, but she wanted to seek something. That night she made a choice; she was not going to die. She gulps down a glass of water with ease and shuffles back up to her bedroom, falling back into bed.

Senora wakes to the sound of a crow cawing outside her bedroom window. "Ok, I'm up already," she says reluctantly. As she slowly makes her way down the stairs, she can hear her mom barking out her words over the phone. "What do you mean you are not coming home? What's so important at work that you're so freely blowing us off? Yes, I know, but." Mom busies herself with unloading the dishwasher. "Wait. Hear me out." She places the plates in the cupboard and sighs. "Are you serious? This is not about work. This is about you." She slams the cupboard door shut. "Wait. I didn't mean it that way." Her mom slams the phone down on the counter as Senora enters the kitchen.

"Mom?" Her mom looks up at Senora with surprise.

"Nora! I didn't know you were up yet. What did you hear?" Her mom looks worried.

"Let me guess, dad has to work and is not coming home tonight."

"Oh Nora, I'm sorry. He does love you."

"I thought he did. But each business trip he takes seems to lead to a new one. Mom, I'm wondering if he'll ever come home. It seems like all he cares about is work."

"At least he's paying the bills."

"Yeah, but money isn't everything. I need him, mom. You need him. Not just to provide but to comfort" She remembers being enveloped in her dad's warm embrace, feeling safe and comforted as he mended her wound and dried her tears after she fell off her bike. With what happened with Trevor, it saddens her to see the pain in her mom's eyes whenever his name is even mentioned. She doesn't think she could put her mom through that much pain again. Life has changed so much since Trevor died. "You know what? Just forget it." Senora turns and stomps to the door.

"Nora, wait," her mom says, pleading for her to stay.

Senora looks over her shoulder and glares.

"Whatever." She pulls open the door, grabs her coat, jumps off the old porch, and runs to the nearby beach. She climbs upon a large rock, sits and watches the waves. She admires how the waves come rolling over the sand and washes the smaller rocks into the sea. She hugs her knees to her chest and brushes a small curl behind her ear to get it out of her eyes. She feels lost in a dream as she remembers Trevor's adventurous spirit. How he stood up for everyone he knew. How he never stood for treating anyone badly.

"Nora, come in for breakfast!" Senora is startled back to the present as she hears her mom calling. She looks over her shoulder, past waves of long grassy fields. Her mom is standing on the back porch of their old, wooden, two-story house. She dries her hands off on her grey apron that she has neatly tied around her waist. A busy day of baking lies ahead of her mom. She bakes so much these days and sells it all at the local farmer's market. As her mom turns, she ties her brown hair back in a tight ponytail. Senora looks down at the large rock she's sitting on and picks up a smaller rock. She inspects its intricate shape, so many different curves and points. As the sun catches it, the rock's surface illuminates a dazzling display of colour. "Nora, now, please," her mom yells once again.

Senora nods, stands up, and dusts her hands off on her torn and faded blue jeans. She takes a deep breath as she tosses the rock into the sea. The waves catch the little rock with a splash and carry it away. *I wish the waves could carry me away too.* She thinks as she turns, jumps off the large rock, and runs through the tall grass to her house.

The door hinges creak as Senora pushes open the door. "Finally! Are you in a better mood? What were you doing?" her mom says from the kitchen. She walks to the entry as Senora pulls off her running shoes and hangs up her black leather jacket.

"Sorry, mom, I didn't mean to snap at you. I was just thinking." Senora shrugs her shoulders as she turns on her heels to face her mom.

"Hmmm, I see. You seem to do that a lot lately. What is it you think about all the time?"

"Just have a lot to think about. Maybe one day, when I can make sense of things and I can explain it better, I will let you know. But for now, just trust me." Senora walks over and kisses her mom's forehead.

"Of course I trust you, Nora. Now come eat your eggs." The two enter the kitchen and sit down at the table to eat their breakfast together.

"Mom, I think I need to clear my head for a while. Can I go for a bike ride after we clean up breakfast?" Senora asks.

"I suppose so, dear. Remember Jo comes home from camp this evening. Make sure you are home for supper."

Senora quickly finishes up her last few bites of eggs and puts her dishes in the dishwasher. "Thanks, mom. I will be home before Jo arrives." Senora pulls on her shoes and coat, turns, and smiles slightly at her mom. She buckles her bike helmet on and opens the door to grab her bike.

The breeze blows past her ears as she peddles down the gravel road. The more memories that pound in her mind, the faster she peddles. She rides around the ocean shores for what seems like hours before turning back towards home. As she pulls back up to the house, her mind is fresh and clear. Senora opens the door and kicks off her shoes. "Mom, I'm back."

"Great, that was a long ride. Did you enjoy yourself?" her mom asks.

"It was much needed and refreshing. Thanks, mom." Senora smiles slightly.

"I am glad it helped. Now, can you set the table? Your brother should be home soon." Senora slumps her shoulders in protest as she reaches into the cupboard to pull out three plates and lay them gently on the table. Her spirit leaps a little for excitement at the thought of seeing Josiah again. He has been away for almost the whole summer; she could hardly contain her excitement to have him back.

As she places the last plate on the table she can hear the rumbling of Josiah's truck coming down the gravel road. Senora looks through the dusty window as Josiah's truck screeches to a halt, and his door flies open. She runs to the door and opens it to see Josiah juggling two large, duffle bags which instantly crash to the ground as Senora runs out the door and hugs him. "Welcome home, big bro!" As she pulls away to compose herself, she punches Josiah in the right shoulder.

"Ow! What was that for?" Josiah rubs his shoulder.

"For staying away all summer."

"You know I was counseling at camp. But I'm here now."

"Now, now, you two. Supper will get cold. Come and eat." They follow their mom into the dining room and sit to eat their supper.

As Senora slurps down her last bite of spaghetti, she coughs to clear her throat. "So, Jo, have you talked much with dad this summer?"

"You haven't? I guess a little, but I was pretty busy at camp and he was probably busy with work too. Thanks, mom, for supper. It was great to finally have a home-cooked meal. I feel like it has been forever, but can I be excused, so I can unpack and bring my things to my room?" She dismisses him with a gentle wave, and he heads out to get his duffle bags. Senora clears the table and helps her mom load the dishwasher. Josiah returns to the front door balancing his duffle bags and carefully navigates his way up the rickety, old stairs.

"Mom, I'm going upstairs for a while. I'll talk to you later. I'm tired." Senora turns before her mom can protest and runs up the stairs to her room. Not much later, she's staring out the window, deep in thought once more.

The kids at school are either mean to her, or they treat her like she's not even there. She wrestles with her own thoughts. She feels like a funny looking, skinny, but fat person, who talks too much. She's unlovable and too nice. Each word hits her like an avalanche of hateful memories.

She remembers her dad's mottos: "It's not worth doing unless you put your whole heart into it," "Only losers give up," and "We are not to surrender." Dad is the strongest man she knows, and she would never trade him for anyone else. They may not always see eye-to-eye, but no matter what choices she has made over the years, at least the important choices, he's always her biggest supporter. He is human and yes, he has made his fair share of mistakes. But she loves him and nothing would ever change that.

Tomorrow starts a new year of school for Senora. "I hope that it'll be a good one. Maybe, just maybe, grade 10 will be easier." Senora gives herself a little pep talk as she drifts off to sleep.

She wakes to the bus honking its horn outside her window. She quickly jumps out of bed, gets dressed, runs down the stairs, grabs her backpack, and bolts out the door. She gasps as she receives a face full of dust as the bus drives away. "No, wait. I'm here." Her words trail away as the bus disappears from sight around the bend.

The door creaks open from behind her. "Way to go, missed the bus on the first day, eh?" She turns to see Josiah leaning on the door frame behind her. She takes a deep breath, swallows her pride, and looks her brother straight in his eyes. "Could you give me a ride today, by any chance?"

"I suppose, just this once. But don't make it a habit. Can't be seen with a lowly grade tenner all the time." Josiah says with a twinkle in his eyes.

Senora rolls her eyes, climbs into his truck, and slams the door. Josiah saunters slowly over to the driver's side and opens his door. "You're welcome."

Senora folds her arms, nods, "thanks." Josiah shakes his head, laughs, and starts the truck. *Oh great, what a wonderful way to start my grade 10 year.* She slumps in her seat.

Most of her life she befriends people who tell her outright that she's never going to amount to anything, that she should give up, or that she's stupid. These words not only come from her peers, but they come from teachers too. She tells herself not to give into these hurts; they are lies.

She's pulled from her thoughts as Josiah slams on his brakes outside her school. She swallows her pride once again, "Thanks for the ride." She slowly climbs out of the truck. Josiah drives away quickly to park. "Here we go again. School this year is starting out with so many hurts, confusion, and pain." Knowing that she starts this year without Trevor fills her heart with sadness, knowing that he isn't just a phone call away at college, brings tears to her eyes. Why didn't he talk to her? Why didn't he share his internal battle with someone else? Why did Robert's dad have his guns unlocked that day? So many questions need answers as she heads to her first class of the day.

Down the hallway, she can see Robert shoving another kid into the lockers, trip a kid to the floor, and rip another kid's book from their hands. "Oops, clumsy me. You might want to watch where you're going." Robert laughs. Senora quickly turns into her classroom before he notices her. She has to remember to avoid him because her anger and pain is too great right now. Will it ever go away?

She breathes a sigh of relief when the final bell of the day rings. She gathers her books and quickly makes her way to the bus. "Thank goodness, I managed a full day without seeing...." She suddenly falls to the ground. Her knee aches at the pain as it skins on the sidewalk.

"Hey, Nora." She cringes at the sound of Robert's voice.

She quickly stands, turns on her heel, and stares him square in the eyes. "You're getting on my nerves."

"At least you're noticing me now." Robert chuckles.

"What's that supposed to mean?" Senora folds her hands in front of her.

"Have you been avoiding me?"

"Maybe. Look, I need to get on the bus." She turns and starts to climb the bus stairs when she feels mud smack into her back. She tries desperately to choke back the frustration as she makes her way to her seat.

She slams the front door shut in anger, throws her books down the hallway, and kicks her shoes in different directions. "I hate school. I am never going back," she screams out to anyone who will listen, and she stomps up the stairs to her bedroom and slams the door. She quickly throws off her shirt and pulls on a new one as she falls onto her bed in a flood of tears; she hears a gentle knock on the door. "Whoever it is, go away," she yells harshly at the door.

The door slowly opens, "Nora? What's wrong? Do you want to talk about it?" her mom asks calmly.

"Oh, what's the use?" She mumbles into her pillow. "Robert's just mean. I try to be nice to him, and he calls me names. Then, you know me, I react. I call him an idiot and tell him to stop being a loser. But no matter what I do, he gets worse every day."

She feels her mom gently stroke her back as she presents her case. She's always there to listen without any judgment. "Now I'm not making excuses for Bobbie, but you do understand his parents are facing a divorce right now. You used to be friends; maybe it's easier for him to get his aggression out at you because you're safe?"

Senora lifts her tear-filled eyes towards her mom. "Don't defend him. I'm not his friend. That was Trevor. Robert is just plain rude. He literally threw mud at my back. Mom, he's the one who needs to grow up. I'm done." A twinge of regret creeps up in her throat as she sees the tears well up in her mom's eyes.

Through her pillows she says, "I'm sorry. I don't want to make you feel sad. I'm just tired of being ignored and feeling invisible."

"What do you mean?"

She slowly lifts her eyes off the pillow enough to see her mom's face. "Well, on the one hand, the kids at school just ignore me. It makes me feel invisible, like they wish I never existed, and on the other hand, Robert sees me but only to make fun of me and call me names. It makes me feel worthless."

"Oh Nora, growing up is so hard. One thing you need to ask yourself is who defines who you are? Do the kids at school? Does Bobbie? Do I? Does your dad? Does God? Only you can answer that question. What you believe you are is what will come out in your actions and your words."

She hears the front door open as Josiah quietly enters. "Please leave me alone. I need some time," Senora says.

Her mom slowly rises from the bed and pauses slightly at the door. "Who are you really, Nora?" she asks quietly before she closes the door behind her. Senora can hear her mom's footsteps as her mom walks down the stairs to greet her brother.

"Honestly, I don't know who I am." Senora's words hang in the air almost to taunt her.

She hears the doorbell ring. "Package for a Miss Senora and Mr. Josiah Fredrickson." The mailman's voice reaches her from the bottom of the stairs. Senora slowly makes her way down the hallway and down the stairs. Josiah meets her at the bottom stair. "What is it, Mom?" Josiah asks.

"It's from your father. Here, Jo, Nora, see what he has sent you." Mom encourages them as she hands each one their brown-wrapped boxes.

As Senora tears through the wrapping, her hopes sink as she pulls out a leather-bound Treasure Kingdom book and a note that says. "I know how you like to tell stories. Maybe you and I can read this story together when I get back."

When will that happen? Dad is never home long enough for that, she thinks.

"Really! A flashlight? I could have used that at camp, but now?" Josiah asks.

"Jo, Nora, can you put your gifts away and come wash up for dinner?" Mom returns to the dining room. Josiah clips the flashlight to his belt loop and heads to the bathroom, leaving Senora holding this dumb old book. She grabs her backpack and shoves the book in to get it out of the way. As she turns to head in the direction of the bathroom, she's startled when she hears a faint humming noise.

"What? Who's there?" As she walks toward the entry, Jo comes out of the bathroom.

"No procrastinating, Nora. It's your turn to wash up. See you at the table," he says as he turns and walks to the dining room.

She rolls her eyes and nods over her shoulder at Josiah. The humming gets louder. "Hello?" she says again as she reaches the front door. "Hello?" She looks around, confused, but all is silent. She shrugs her shoulders and goes to wash up; there is a slight glow in Senora's backpack as the humming starts and slowly fades away again.

CHAPTER 2

God's Strength

Senora walks through blooming fields of dandelions. Josiah looks around to get his bearings, and hears, "Josiah.... Josiah...," it was a soft, faint whisper, carried on the breeze.

"Who's there?" Josiah turns around curiously, and he notices Senora picking some flowers and skipping through the field. It's definitely not Senora who's calling him. "Who's there? Nora, do you hear that?" Still, Senora continues through the field as if she doesn't hear him.

His eyes are blinded briefly with a flash of light. The sound of ringing penetrates his ears, hearing a blood curdling growl. Falling to his knees, he feels blind and disoriented.

"Jo, are you alright?" He hears Senora's voice. Josiah's spot filled eyes blink to try to focus on his sister. As she comes into view, he sees her running toward him. His face starts to sweat as the temperature starts to rise. When Senora is only five steps away from him he sees a flash of silver from behind her.

"Nora, look out," he says.

Senora stops suddenly and slowly starts to turn her head.

"You're no help to anyone," a loud voice echoes in his ears and flames engulf the ground.

All goes black and Josiah sits up in his bed, beads of sweat dripping off his brow. He looks around, but no one is there. It was only a dream. He stands up and walks down the hall, pausing at his sister's door. He hears her gentle snoring. "Good, all is quiet, she's safe."

Josiah gets a drink of water from the kitchen. As he turns to head back up the stairs, he sees a dim glow by the front door, and he hears humming. *Where is that coming from?* He thinks to himself as he walks towards the light. It seems to be coming from Senora's backpack. When he picks up the backpack the light goes out and the humming stops. He quickly drops it. "That was strange." He picks up the backpack and hangs it back on the wall hook and turns back up the stairs.

As his head rests on the pillow, sleep overtakes him again. Josiah finds himself wandering through a thick forest. "I have to find Nora, before it's too late." He hears footsteps running behind him and instinct takes over. Taking a deep breath, he crashes through tree branches, and soon his lungs burn with the smoke that surrounds him. The trees are full of flames. As he runs frantically searching for Senora, his foot trips over a fallen tree branch.

"Jo, look out," Senora yells out a warning before he falls. The flames lick at the tree trunks around him, and he feels dizzy and confused. Senora comes into view through the smoke.

"Hang on, Jo." As the sight fades from view he hears gunfire. "Are you strong enough?"

Senora's voice hangs in his thought as he opens his eyes to the sunlight streaming into his bedroom window. The visions of these two dreams are still fresh in his mind. His forehead is still sweating at the thought of the raging fire. What do they mean? Why am I so scared that something bad is going to happen to Senora? Question after question races through his mind. He quickly gets dressed and heads downstairs where Mom is cooking breakfast.

"Hey Jo, you look like you've seen a ghost." Mom laughs.

"Oh, just strange dreams." He goes over to the counter and pours himself a cup of coffee.

"Jo, I know it is not really your thing, but I have a meeting tonight. I am worried about Nora. She seems to be dealing with a lot lately. Can you take her out, while I am in the meeting?"

Josiah groans. He's not sure if he wants to be with her tonight. Every time he tries to do anything with her, it ends up in a fight. "As long as Nora doesn't cause issues." He rolls his eyes at his mom.

"She should be fine. She has not been the same since Trevor died. She doesn't talk about him, but always seems lost in thought. I know we all miss him, but I worry she might make the same choices he did."

"Don't say that Mom; what happened to Trevor was a mistake. It was not anyone's fault."

"She will not talk to me. Can you please try?" his mom asks. He knows losing Trevor was hard on all of them, but Trevor should have talked to someone. "She also seems to be having some issues lately with Bobbie. Do you know anything about this?" she looks at Josiah, concerned.

Josiah takes one more sip of his coffee and says, "Bobbie? I guess he does tend to speak before he thinks, but so does Nora. Could just be a personality clash."

He remembers sitting at a table, having his lunch in the school cafeteria when Bobbie approaches him. "Hey Jo, how's your day goin?" Bobbie slaps Josiah on the shoulder.

"Hey Bobbie, I am hanging in there. You?"

"I have a little confession to make." Josiah cringes, not sure how to prepare himself for what Bobbie will say next. You never know. "You see, I have a little crush on someone."

"Wow, I didn't see that one coming. Why tell me?"

"Well, you see she has such gumption and spunk, I don't want to scare her away, but I do want her to know who I am."

"I say again, why tell me? It's not like we're close or anything."

Bobbie punches Josiah's shoulder. "Hey now, don't be mean. I'm trying to be civil here! Now hear me out. Will ya?" Unsure where he's going with this, he nods for him to continue. "She makes me want to be better, but with everything that has happened lately, ya know with Trevor and all, she looks at me with such disgust."

"Wait. Let me stop you there. What does Trevor have to do with this?"

"Well, Trevor would help me know how to talk with her. Now he's gone."

"Soooo, Trevor knew this girl?"

"Ok, I confess. I like your sister, Nora."

"You what? Why?"

"What do you mean, why? You know, just forget it. I knew you wouldn't understand. I will get her attention one way or another." Bobbie storms away.

Personally, Josiah doesn't see anything fancy about Senora. But then again, she's his younger sister. It's funny that when they were younger, people thought they were twins. Josiah thought she was very immature, and if anyone knows them, they would see that Josiah was clearly older.

"I have baseball practice after school, so I will be a little late getting home, what time is your meeting?" Josiah says to his mom.

"7:00 pm."

"Ok, I'll be home by 5:00. Don't worry; I'll take Nora out for coffee or something. I have to head to school, love you, Mom." Josiah finishes his last sip of coffee, gives his mom a hug and kiss on the cheek. As he leaves the house, Senora comes down the stairs, hearing Josiah's truck pull away. She wishes she had spares so they could ride together, but she is also glad he doesn't ride with her because they would probably fight.

"Oh, Nora, good you're up. I have a meeting to go to tonight; Jo is going to take you to the Diner."

Senora rubs the sleep from her eyes. She slowly reaches for a cereal bowl.

"What sort of meeting?"

"Just a meeting at the church."

"Do I have to go with Jo? I'm 15, and I don't need a babysitter anymore, Mom." Senora scowls at her mom.

"You said it yourself that you missed him over the summer. This will give him a chance to share with you what he learned."

"Oh, goodie." Rolling her eyes, she gives up and says, "Fine, I'll go." She is curious about what he did all summer. It might be fun. If not, at least she will get free french fries. She chuckles to herself as she takes a few bites of her cereal. "Do I have to go to school today?"

"Nora, you know school is important."

"But what do I do about Robert?"

"Just try to avoid him. He's in a higher grade than you, so at lunch time just don't go where he hangs out."

"Fine, I'll try!" Senora grabs her backpack as she hears the bus pulling up. "I will see you after school." She runs out the door and climbs aboard the bus. Senora finds a seat in the back to sit by herself and looks out the window. Trevor would have understood and stuck up for her. He didn't like school either. She sure does miss him. He listened, unlike Josiah.

"Nora…" She jumps at the sound of her name, she looks around but the three other kids on the bus are sitting more in the front. They are all laughing and talking with each other. "Nora…" She looks around again wondering who is calling her.

She notices that her backpack has something glowing inside it. She can hear quiet humming. She unzips her backpack and slowly reaches in. Other than her lunch, the only thing she pulls out is that dumb, old book her dad gave her. She forgot she had it in there. As she looks at it, she notices that the binding is a little loose. When she opens the front cover a silver necklace falls into her lap. What's this? She picks it up and notices it has a silver pendant on it in the shape of an eagle. It glows slightly, or was that her imagination? The bus slows as it approaches the school. She quickly shoves the book back into her backpack and puts the necklace around her neck.

As Josiah makes his way down the hallway towards his first class he hears footsteps running up behind him. Before he can turn to see who it is, he feels a fist plunge into his left shoulder. "Hey loser. Long time no see."

Josiah rubs his shoulder and looks over at Bobbie. "What was that for?"

"Just sayin hi. Trevor never minded. Don't be a wimp. You're cramping my style."

A lump forms in Josiah's throat at the sound of his brother's name. Why does Bobbie have to bring him up? The memory of what happened to Trevor still haunts him.

"Hey, did Nora mention me?"

"Only that you pick on her. Can you just lay off? You aren't her type anyways."

"Oh, you'll see. She at least knows who I am now. All part of the plan."

"Hey, that is my little sister you're talkin about." Josiah clenches his fist.

Bobbie gets right in his face, "What are you going to do?" Josiah wants to hit Robert, but calms down and takes a deep breath. "Ha! That's what I thought. You should stop gettin mad over small things," Bobbie scoffs at him. "Do ya always take everything so personally? I mean, come on. Why can't ya just laugh it off and move on?" Josiah takes a few breaths to subside his frustration. Why does he have to be so harsh? "Anyways," Bobbie punches Josiah's left shoulder again, "I have to head to class. Don't be so sensitive. Later, loser." Bobbie turns, shifts direction, and walks away laughing.

How can Josiah be there for everyone? He couldn't even save Trevor. He thought he knew him, but the Trevor he knew would never have a gun. If he could see the pain the whole family is in now, things would be different, at least he hopes it would have been different. He pushes his own feelings aside; he needs to be strong for everyone else. If not, his family will fall apart. Look at Bobbie's family. Bobbie acts like he can handle anything. He will not back down and he will fight for his life and his mom's. His dad was put in prison for armed robbery, less than six months ago. Bobbie says it is a good thing, that way he's not a punching bag for his dad. Josiah knows Bobbie blames his dad for what happened with Trevor, and with how poorly he has treated him and his mom, but Josiah doesn't know what to do. Bobbie's hurting, but he also doesn't seem to care. Josiah feels like he's being pulled from all directions. The bell rings for class to start. Josiah squares his shoulders and pushes his thoughts aside. No time for this now; he needs to focus.

—◦◦◦—

"Hey, you ok?" Josiah asks with concern in his voice as Senora enters the school cafeteria.

"I'm fine." She pushes aside the frustration, confusion, and guilt that is bombarding her right now. He always seems so overprotective. She hates the fact that he's there for everyone.

He's not perfect, but some days, Senora feels so jealous of him. Everything seems to come easily for him. *Why do thing seem so hard for me?* she thinks, as she quickly wipes one last tear from her eye before Josiah can notice. She knows if he sees it, he will start in on his 20-question interrogation. She's in no mood for that right now.

"Would you like to go to the Diner with me tonight?" Josiah asks.

"Do I really have a choice?" Senora doesn't really want to go, but feels pressured into accepting his invitation.

"Come on, you can order anything you want and it's on me." Josiah grins expectantly.

"I'll think about it. What time do you get home from baseball practice?" Senora asks.

"Around five o'clock."

"Look, I have to go before you know who shows up. I will let you know at five if I will go," Senora instructs as she shuffles quickly out of the cafeteria towards her next class.

"But, aren't you going to eat you lunch?" Josiah says

"Just lost my appetite, I know Robert will be here soon. I am in no mood to see him." Senora says over her shoulder.

"Well, are you coming?" Josiah pulls her out of her own thoughts as he holds the door open for her.

"Coming where?"

"To the Diner. We haven't talked for a while. Maybe I can tell you about camp or something." Senora squares her shoulders and fixes her eyes on Josiah's truck outside. She gives a nod of thank you to Josiah as he follows her out the door.

The sun glints off the windshield as the white truck rumbles to a stop at the local Diner. Both doors burst open and Senora and Josiah jump out, hitting the ground running. His long strides easily put him paces ahead of Senora. She pushes hard to catch up, her eyes fixed on his back as he runs up to the Diner door.

Josiah holds the door open for Senora to walk through, "You can pick where we sit." She looks around the old, dusty Diner and sees an empty booth towards the back of the room. She fixes her eyes and walks towards it to sit down; Josiah follows quietly, sitting down across the table from her.

The waitress walks up to their table. "Whatcha havin?"

"I will have a plate of French fries and an iced tea."

"I'll just have a coffee."

"You got it. Be back in a flash." The waitress turns on her heels and heads back into the kitchen area.

"So, what is it you wanted to talk about?" Senora studies Josiah's expression but he is always so hard to read. "Come on, I know there's something on your mind."

"I hear you have a lot on your mind too. Anything you want to talk about?"

Typical Josiah, always turning things around on her. "You're changing the subject. I know that the only reason you took me out tonight is because Mom asked you to. Am I right?"

Josiah scratches the back of his head, "Partly, but I do want to know what you did all summer."

"Yeah, sure. I was stuck at home bored while you were off gallivanting. Dad was off on his worldly travels with work; Mom was crying herself to sleep every night! What do you think I did?" Before he can answer the waitress returns with the drinks.

"Enjoy," she says as she fills up Josiah's coffee cup. She turns and walks away.

"So, camp. How was it?" Senora tries desperately to break the silence.

"Ummm, yeah." Josiah scratches the back of his head again. "It was good, did some mountain climbing, horseback

24

riding, and even got in some archery. One week I was put in charge of teaching the kids how to canoe."

"You? Teach? That's funny! How was that?"

Josiah takes a few sips of his coffee. "Let's just say, I was only on that option for a week. It was interesting."

"How was mountain climbing?"

"I learned how to secure my anchor and how to belay down a cliff safely."

"That sounds like fun."

"It really was I enjoyed mountain climbing."

The waitress returns once more and places Senora's plate of fries down in the middle of the table. "Enjoy," she says as she walks to a different table to take another order.

The bell rings as the door opens, "Oh great! He's the last person I want to see right now." Senora groans as Robert stops behind Josiah.

"Who?" Josiah turns to see, and Robert punches him in the shoulder.

"Hey, I didn't know you were going to be here." Why Josiah would want to even talk with big, dumb, Robert is beyond Senora. He's plain mean. She fixes her eyes on Robert, crosses her arms, and glares. Robert reaches over and takes a handful of her fries and shoves them into his mouth. "Thanks for sharing, Nora." He shoves his way into the booth next to Josiah. "Whatcha all talkin about?"

"None of your business," Senora snaps at him.

"Whatever. I was just pickin up some pizza for supper. Check ya later. Oh, and one more for the road." He grabs another handful of Senora's fries, slaps Josiah on the back, and walks to the till to pick up his pizza. Sometimes Senora wants to put him in his place. He acts like he knows it all and doesn't want to listen to anyone. Josiah rubs his back a little.

"Why do you even hang around him?"

"Well, he was Trevor's friend."

"How dare you! You don't deserve to even mention his name."

"What do you mean, Nora?"

"Look! You don't know what it has been like this summer. Dad has been away. You were gone camping. Who's the one who heard mom cry herself to sleep every night? *Me*."

"What do you mean, cry herself to sleep? She seems so calm."

"That's what she wants us to think. But I know the truth. Before Trevor died, Dad and I were so close, but it's as if he doesn't even know me anymore."

"Now that's not fair."

"Not fair! No, what's not fair is you leaving all summer and hiding at camp and Dad, taking this job away from home. Leaving me to try and hold things together and pick up the pieces that Trevor tore apart."

"Nora, can you please calm down? People are staring."

"Who cares if people are staring? You're always so concerned about what other people think of you."

"Why do you think Dad doesn't know you anymore?"

She reaches into her backpack and pulls out the old book and drops it on the table next to her fries. "He gets you a flashlight and me this dumb book."

"Nora, please lower your voice."

"No, Jo. Why won't you just listen to me? I knew this was a mistake. Nobody in this family or this dumb town understands. No matter what I say or how I act, nobody seems to understand me. Just leave me alone." She grabs the book, storms out of the Diner, and runs into the trees growing alongside the building. "I hate this dumb town. I miss Trevor, but it doesn't seem to matter what I feel or think." She spins around and throws the book at the tree. "Why a book?" She hears that humming again, and looking down, she sees the necklace around her neck, glowing. "Stupid necklace." She breaks the chain and throws it at the book. It disappears.

Senora is suddenly surrounded by a blinding bright light. Her vision is blurred, and these words flash before her eyes:

There are many different moments in our lives,
moments of great laughter and adventure,
and moments of great sorrow and many tears.
But each new moment brings a lesson.
It's our choice on how we will receive these lessons in life.

Senora smells the fragrance of the trees and can hear the leaves rustling in the wind. The wind feels colder. When she opens her eyes she's no longer by the Diner but surrounded by many more birch trees. The humming becomes clearer. Someone's singing. It's not a song she recognizes, but it's beautiful. Senora stands up and slowly pushes away branches as she moves closer to the sound. She sees movement up ahead.

Senora moves forward and peers through the trees. She sees a beautiful girl dressed in a brown leather jacket and black leggings. She is spinning in circles and jumping in the air as her auburn hair sways and dances with her movements, each strand catches the sunlight as she skates rhythmically in figure eights. She is singing a sweet and enchanting tune that Senora cannot make out.

Senora steps cautiously closer to see if she can get a better look. While she watches this girl, Senora starts to feel sleepy and sits down.

Her eyes feel heavy, she yawns and rubs them. As her head bobs a little, she asks, "why do I feel so sleepy?" She yawns again. She gives into her desire to sleep, resting her head on a nearby stone and slowly drifts off.

CHAPTER 3

Tree of Hope: The Path of Friendship

Josiah stands to go looking for Senora, hoping she's alright. Their mom and dad seem to take her side of things. Why does he have to be the bad guy? He wants them all to get along and stop fighting, but it never seems to happen that way. He gets so jealous of her sometimes; being the middle child in the family, he feels that he is the most forgotten. He misses Trevor and he is jealous of the fond memories Senora has of Trevor. They were so close, and Trevor always seemed to know the right words to say to Senora. Josiah wants his voice heard, for her to listen to him and not interrupt all the time. "I don't understand," Josiah says as he thinks about Senora's outburst. What could he have done differently? Could he have done or said something better? He reaches into his pocket and throws some money onto the table to cover their order. "Nora should have calmed down now. I should go and find her."

Josiah exits the Diner and looks around for his sister. "Nora! Nora! Where are you Nora? Are you hiding?" Josiah looks among the trees, but he only hears the wind gently blowing and the birds singing. Then, he finds the open book lying on the ground. "Nora!" Fear takes over, but where is she? She didn't like the book, but she would never just leave it like this. He picks up the open book and sees a picture of what looks like Senora sleeping. He reads under the picture these words:

> *Nora is captured. You must follow the trail*
> *and discover the truth of the Greatest Treasure.*

Josiah scratches the back of his head as he looks around once more. He looks closer at the picture. It definitely is Senora. What is this? What should he do? Is Senora playing a trick on him because she's angry? It does sound like her. He can't tell Mom. If Senora is gone, it will break her. She's still mourning the loss of Trevor, so he can't do that to her. Not now. "Nora, if this is one of your jokes, it's not funny! Where are you?" He can hear the gentle humming. When he looks at the page again, the picture changes and he sees a young girl skating on a frozen pond. The picture appears to be moving. The caption below reads:

> *As sharp as the blade cuts through the ice,*
> *how sharp is your mind to find the prize?*

The book falls from his hands. As he feels the blood drain from his face, he closes his eyes. The vision of Senora picking flowers and the flames flood his mind. When he reopens his eyes, he finds himself standing in the ruins of an old building. "Hello? Is anyone here? Where am I?" His voice echoes all around him. He fears that he is all alone.

The building Josiah is standing in is completely made of large stones cemented together. There are large rectangular holes, indicating that the windows are missing. Another large hole stands where there once had been a door. There's no ceiling at all. Senora is missing, and now, he's in a strange place. Not only does he have to worry about Senora, but how is Mom going to feel when she finds both of them missing? He starts to worry about his sister and fears for her safety flood his mind. Suddenly he hears rustling coming from outside. Without even thinking, he runs out to see if, maybe, Senora is waiting to jump out and scare him. It would be so like her.

At the entrance, a tall, bearded man comes into view, and Josiah is startled by his sudden appearance. The man stands with authority, tall as a tree, with a wavy, red beard on his square chin, and a gentle wrinkle at the edges of his kind, blue eyes. They appear to be filled with wisdom. Josiah stares expectantly, waiting for him to speak.

The man raises his hand. "Do not be afraid. I will not hurt you, Jo."

A shiver runs down Josiah's spine.

"Yyyessssir" he says with fear, stumbling over his words. "How do you know me? Who are you? Do you know where my sister is?"

"I saw you in the Diner with your sister, Nora."

The thought of his sister makes Josiah fill with fear.

"Jo, don't allow fears power over you. Nora's safe."

"Where's my sister? Have you taken her?"

"Jo, I haven't taken her, but I can tell you that she's safe, at least for now."

"What do you mean, for now? I don't understand."

"I know you both have been through a lot. You miss Trevor."

"How do you know that?"

"I know that you love both your siblings. You couldn't save Trevor, but you can save Nora. It's not too late. I can help point you in the right direction, but you have to trust me."

"Why should I trust you? I don't know who you are."

"I know you're hurting, but your sister's hurting too. She needs your help."

"Help? I thought you said she was safe. You're not making sense."

The man looks at Josiah with his gentle eyes. He doesn't appear to be dangerous, but he also seems to know a lot about Josiah, but he knows nothing about the stranger, or how he got there. "I know you're confused right now and you hold many unanswered questions. I promise you that if you choose to take this journey, you will find your sister, but you both will not be the same. With a time for everything, you need to trust. So remember no matter how hard things get, there's always light somewhere. Even if it may be small, it's always there. Once you find that light, hold onto it because darkness will always flee from the light and in turn that small light will grow. Job 33:29 says 'Behold, God does all these things, twice, three times, with a man, to bring back his soul from the pit, that he may be lighted with the light of life.'

The man points his long finger towards a strange-looking tree. "Your journey starts there. Go beyond the Tree of Hope. You will find some answers, and more instructions will follow. 'The Lord gives power to the faint, and to him who has no might, He increases strength; but they who wait for the Lord shall renew their strength; they shall mount up with wings like eagles; they shall run and not be weary; they shall walk and not faint.[1]"

Josiah looks towards the tree as the man speaks, lost in his own thoughts. *I can trust this man. Although he's mysterious, I can trust him. I must find Nora.*

"How will I know the way?" Josiah asks, but when he turns back, the man is gone.

---

[1]   Isaiah 40:29-31

"Okay, Josiah," he says to himself. "What choice do you have? I have nothing else to lose. Tree of Hope, here I come."

———❧———

Senora wakes up and finds herself in a bedroom. Reaching up to remove a cloth from her forehead, she sits up in a bed. Looking around, she sees one large window off to one side with a closet in the same corner. The walls are painted yellow which makes the room feel peaceful and cheery. There is a small white dresser sitting in the corner of the room. She shivers with a chill that hangs in the air. "Where am I?" she whispers to herself. Nothing looks familiar, "Where did that beautiful girl go?" Suddenly, the bedroom door flies open with a bang. She's startled and jumps so high she nearly falls out of bed.

Senora looks towards the now-open door where a young woman stands holding a tray in her hands. As the woman walks, she appears to float on air, seeming to hardly be touching the floor. "Oh good, you're awake." Her voice is soft and peaceful. The woman sets a tray of food down beside Senora and checks Senora's forehead with a little concern flickering in her eyes. "I was beginning to think you would never wake up."

"Who are you?" Senora asks, but the woman doesn't answer. The woman busies herself with tidying the room. She's only a few inches taller than Senora, with long fiery red hair, thin lips. Smooth and silent, she moves around the room, like an angel might. After a few minutes of cleaning, she stops and stares at Senora with her deep, emerald green eyes.

"I found you asleep in the Forgetful Woods. Why were you there? Wait, did he bring you there? I mean, I don't want any trouble."

"Who? Nobody took me there. Who are you talking about?" Senora asks.

"He brings his enemies there to forget. Nobody has been there since," the woman begins as she stares off into nothingness, letting her words fade away.

"Since what?" Senora asks curiously.

"Not important, not important." She says and gives Senora a hug. "Eat up. You will need your strength." She turns on her heels and leaves the room as quickly as she entered.

Confused, Senora climbs out of bed and eats a few bites of toast. After a few minutes, she tiptoes to the doorway, walks through, and finds herself entering a large open living room. Beautiful couches line the walls, and sunlight shines through the windows. "Hello?" Senora says.

"Oh, good. You're up." The woman appears from around a corner. "Did you eat enough?"

"Yes, thank you. Where am I?" Senora asks the woman again.

"Not important, not important," The woman repeats. The woman stares out a window and says, "Where shall I go from your spirit? Or where shall I go from your presence? If I ascend to heaven, you are there! If I make my bed in the darkness of death, you are there! If I take the wings of the morning and dwell in the uttermost parts of the sea, even there your hand shall lead me, and your right hand shall hold me.[2]"

"Who shall guide you?" Senora asks. "I'm confused. Who are you talking about?" The woman looks at Senora and smiles.

"Not important, not important." She says. "You ready?" the woman asks Senora.

"Ummm, ready for what?" Senora asks, confused.

"Your adventure, of course." The woman laughs. She busies herself again filling a backpack with food and clothing. "You must find the Greatest Treasure, and the key."

---

[2]   Psalm 139:7-10

"What are you talking about?" Senora feels even more confused than when she first woke up.

"Do you not know?" the woman asks. "Not important, you need to ask the right questions," the woman says.

"Right questions? What do you mean? I was just in the Diner with my brother." Senora wonders to herself if the woman has mistaken her for someone else.

"Don't be silly. 'For where your treasure is, there your heart will be also.'[3] Let me ask you, what do you treasure the most?"

"What do you mean by Greatest Treasure?" Senora says.

"Never give up hope. Remember, for He has said, 'I will never leave you nor forsake you.'[4]" the woman says.

"Who will never leave me?" Senora asks.

"In time, in time you will see," The woman says. "Now, you must begin. Remember: never give up. The journey is not an easy one. You must go to the Path of Friendship. That's where your journey begins to get to the Peaceful River. That's where you will find him."

"Find who?" Senora says.

"Jo, your brother, of course. You will need each other. You both, together, must discover what the Greatest Treasure is, you must learn as you go and understand who you really are. Now Go." The woman rushes Senora out the door and points in the direction of a pathway that leads through some trees.

"Wait. Jo? He's here too?" Senora says.

The woman places her hands on her hips and lets out a huge sigh "You sure do ask a lot of meaningless questions. The journey and the solution is what are important. Now you must hurry so that your brother will be at the Peaceful River at the same time you arrive. Stop stalling. Follow the way of the Red Dragon." The woman takes Senora by the arm and

---

[3]   Matthew 6:21
[4]   Hebrews 13:5

leads Senora down four steps, turns her toward the start of the path, and gives her a little shove forward. The woman turns on her heels, walks back up the stairs and re-enters the house. She returns to the top of the stairs shortly after. "Hey," She says. Senora turns and looks at the woman over her shoulder. "Here, this might help." The woman tosses Senora the backpack. She picks it up off the ground and puts it on her back. The woman nods her head, turns on her heels, and shuts the door.

Senora's left standing before the pathway, all by herself, feeling confused. She still doesn't understand a word of this strange woman. Her eyes fill with tears as she thinks of both her brothers and the fight that she had with Josiah. She wipes them away and shivers with fear.

She wants to give up already and curl up into a ball, but Senora's reminded of her brother, and she knows that Josiah would do anything to keep her safe. Yeah, they may fight, but she knows he loves her. A piercing roar drops Senora to her knees, she feels a blast of wind. When she finds the courage to look up, she can see a flash of red fly overhead and disappears beyond the tree line. Drawing on the strength that only her love for Josiah can muster, she makes a promise to herself. "I will not lose another brother. I guess I am following a Red Dragon." She nervously steps onto the path.

Josiah shrugs and turns toward the Tree of Hope. He squares his shoulders and takes his first step. "Ok, Josiah, here goes nothing. Never give up. This doesn't seem too hard."

He starts to walk up the hill towards the Tree of Hope. The birds are singing happily in the surrounding trees, and Josiah whistles a little tune for them as he walks. He looks around as he climbs the hill and notices the mountains that surround him. The vastness of the rock statues make him feel small. The wind starts to blow sending a chill down his spine.

The higher he climbs, the stronger the wind blows, and each step takes his breath away. He forgets the tune he was whistling and puts all of his attention on each new step as the hill incline increases and the rocks become more slippery.

"Come on Josiah, you can do this." He gives himself a little pep talk as he stops to catch his breath. "Boy, I didn't realize how steep this hill really is." Josiah brushes the back of his hand across his forehead. He takes off his jacket, ties it around his waist and continues up the hill. As the wind increases, Josiah's ears start to ache in the cold. He stops once more as he places his jacket over his head to protect his ears. He shivers and yet he feels sweaty. "Never give up," he says to himself again.

It starts to rain and as he walks on, the wind blows the rain in his face. He shuffles trying to maintain his footing. His foot slips on a stone, falling to his knees and he falls backwards, "This is hopeless," Josiah says as he tries desperately to regain his balance. "How will I ever find Nora in this cold rain? It's tiring me out."

Never give up, an unknown voice says. "Never give up." A little louder. "Never give up. Never give up." It's Josiah's voice and he yells at the top of his lungs. The man's words echo in his mind: *He gives power to the faint, to the one who has no might, He gives strength.* These words come to him as he remembers what he learned from camp. Josiah stands back on his feet. The rain pounds down upon his head and shoulders.

"Do you not know that in a race all the runners run, but only one receives the prize?" Josiah takes a step forward. "So run that you may obtain it." He takes two more steps. "They shall renew their strength, they shall mount up with wings like eagles." The Tree of Hope comes into view. "They shall run and not be weary." Josiah starts to run. "They shall walk and not be faint."

He can almost touch the tree now, but his knee is throbbing in pain. He runs a few more steps, panting for breath. Just as he reaches out his hand, he falls forward. A rock cuts into his hand and the pain seeps in. Josiah lies on the ground. His knee and hand are bleeding, his head is pounding, and he's gasping for breath. His muscles are aching, and his eyes are heavy. As the rain pounds down upon him, he closes his eyes, feeling his body relax as he drifts into a peaceful sleep.

The rain lightens, and the sun starts to peek through the clouds. Josiah opens his eyes as he feels the warmth of the sunshine reach his back. He finds himself lying face down on rocky ground with his left hand stretched out in front of him. He winces in pain when he tries to move his leg. Standing up, he sees that he is standing right next to the Tree of Hope. A shadow blocks the sun from his eyes, as his eyes adjust to see who is standing over him.

"You show great strength," the tall, bearded man says.

Josiah leans on the tree to get his bearings. He unties his coat from around his ears, pulls a piece of bandana from his coat pocket, and sits at the bottom of the tree. He dabs the bandana on his knee and hand to stop the bleeding. "What sort of journey have you started me on? Do you promise this will lead me to Nora?"

"You will find your sister. 'Now I rejoice in my sufferings for your sake.'[5] 'And the God of all grace, who called you to His eternal glory in Christ, after you have suffered a little while, will Himself restore you and make you strong, firm and steadfast.'[6]"

"I can't give up now," he whispers. His muscles ache from the climb.

---

[5]   Colossians 1:24
[6]   1 Peter 5:10

The sun shines down on him and he notices that his clothes are almost dry now. He looks out over the valley before him. "Do you see that maze of rock?" the man asks Josiah.

Josiah sees mountains and rolling hills. As far as his eyes can see, a valley stretches before him. Large mountains tower above him and the sky is bright blue without a single cloud to be seen. The air feels damp, still carrying the scent of rain.

Far in the distance, he can see giant rocks. There are so many rocks that it looks like a sea of stone slabs. "Where do I go from here?" Josiah asks. He rises to his feet, wincing in pain.

The man stretches out his arm and points at the maze of stones. "It's called the Stone Maze of Knowledge. Your journey is far from over. Be careful as you make your way there. You will have to be strong." The man points his finger over the valley below. "The Abandoned Forest is not always so forgiving. You must go through there, you will be tested, and will your heart be true? To find Nora, you must be wise and find your way through."

"I must continue. I have no choice. I need to find Nora. Well, forward it is. Never give up. Thanks." He nods at the man and begins his slow descent into the valley below him.

Senora enters the forest and walks down the path. "This is going to be easy." Senora sighs to herself. She admires the beautiful flowers growing along the path. They make a rainbow of colours: purple, white, blue, and yellow. Senora's also amazed by the wonderful song the birds are singing.

The wind blows through the trees making the leaves shudder their own song. Memories of dancing in the rain and puddle jumping with Josiah rush into her mind. She's reminded of playing hide-and-seek among the trees with her brothers, and her heart aches when she remembers the fight she had with Josiah. She adjusts the straps on her backpack.

With a deep breath she continues down the path. She's enamoured with her surroundings, but she doesn't watch where she's stepping. Her foot suddenly sinks into a big, gooey puddle. She's stuck! She squirms and pulls, but her foot will not budge. "What am I going to do now?" she asks herself, feeling hopeless. She twists and pushes up with her other foot, but she still cannot get free. In the distance, she sees a young man walking down the path toward her. He's tall with shaggy black hair. His arms look as big as tree trunks and he looks as though he could bench press a bus. *Surely he's strong enough to pull me free,* Senora thinks. "Hello?" she calls to find help. "Can you help me?" The man stops and looks up at her. He looks around as if to see if anyone else is there, and sees that Senora's foot is stuck in the mud.

His lips start to quiver and shake as they turn into a smile. Not a happy smile, but a mischievous and cruel smile. Senora feels a sense of uneasiness rise within her. He starts to laugh at her, "You should see yourself. You look absolutely ridiculous." The man slaps his hand on his hip and laughs. He coughs to clear his throat. "You got yourself into this mess, so you get yourself out."

"But I have…"

"Stop." The man holds up his hand toward Senora. "I don't want to hear any excuses."

Senora looks around, wondering if he's still talking to her or possibly someone else. "I was not going to give excuses. I was simply explaining that I have tried…"

"Stop. I will hear no more of this. You say that you're not trying to make excuses, fine. Then, I don't want to hear any complaining. Kids these days. All they do is make excuses and complain. Well, I have had enough of you. Get yourself out. I'll not bail you out of a mess that you clearly got yourself caught in."

"But…" Senora says, stumbling over her words.

He chuckles. "You know this is funny. You look ridiculous, looking like you have no left foot. That right there is funny." He throws his hands up in the air, slaps his knees, turns around still laughing, and walks back up the path from where he had come.

"No, wait. Come back." Senora yells. Her words fade away as the man disappears. Despair and discouragement well up within her. She pushes away the urge to cry as she realizes that she's alone. She squirms some more, trying to free her foot. She loses her balance and falls over backwards in the mud. She reaches out her hand, grabs her own foot and pulls with all her strength. Her foot will not move. Senora begins to feel like she might be stuck here forever.

A young lady walks toward her in the distance. This girl is slender with long, flowing, light brown hair. She has glasses on her face and carries herself with dignity and grace. "Hello? Can you please help me?" Senora says, trying to get the lady's attention.

The girl looks Senora straight in the eyes with anger and disgust. This is a look Senora knew well and has given her brother, Josiah, often. Senora's heart feels like it'll break, and tears well up in her eyes. "Please help me. I'm stuck, and I cannot get free on my own."

The girl shrugs her shoulders and flips her hair through her fingers. "Stop being a baby." The girl snickers. She folds her arms and leans on a nearby tree. "You got yourself in that mess. You get yourself out."

"Please. I've tried and my foot will not."

"Save it." The girl snaps her fingers.

A wave of desperation wells up within Senora's heart. "Believe me, I am telling you the truth."

"Enough already. Do you even know what truth is?" The girl rolls her eyes and snorts a little. "All people cheat, lie, manipulate. You're nothing. You say you're stuck, but are you really? Or are you just trying to trick me into believing your betrayal?" The girl laughs. "I know what you're doing and I will not help you one bit." She turns on her heels and leaves the same way she had come.

Senora feels a wave of both hopelessness and sadness. "What do I do now?" She sees visions of all the times Robert had called her a baby, pushed her, or laughed at her. She feels sad and hurt. She hides her face in her hands and cries bitterly. "This is hopeless; I'm never going to get out of here," she says through her tears.

Then, she remembers a quote from the Bible. "Your right hand shall hold me, and you shall guide me,[7]" she hears a small whisper on the wind.

She wipes the tears away from her face. "I'm not sure who is holding me."

"If you falter in times of trouble, how small is your strength.[8] Never give up. You're not alone," a still small whisper reaches her ear.

"Please. I may not know who you are or why you're with me, but please send someone who will help." She tries pulling her foot free one more time. "Still stuck and now I'm completely covered in mud."

"Peace I leave with you; my peace I give to you. I do not give to you as the world gives. Do not let your hearts be troubled and do not be afraid.[9]"

As Senora sits, she hears laughter and what sounds like someone jumping on the ground. She looks around, but she cannot tell where it's coming from. It gradually gets louder. Someone must be coming down the path. Soon, the lady from the house comes laughing and skipping over the hill. Her mouth curves in a beautiful, friendly smile. She seems

---

[7]   Psalm 139:7
[8]   Proverbs 24:10
[9]   John 14:27

curious and full of life, but she's still so mysterious, as her movements are soft and smooth. She skips back and forth along the path, as if floating again, stopping to inspect some flowers along the way.

Senora is hesitant to call out to her. How could she help? Then Senora remembers the other two people who had refused to help her. She asks herself, *why would she even want to help me? I cannot get out on my own; I have tried.*

When she is about three feet from Senora, she stops and looks up at her, her green eyes glisten. Senora sees the lady is smiling at her. Senora wonders about this smile. *Is she just going to mock and laugh at me like the others?* She thinks. *No, this is not a smile of mockery at all. It's not even a smile of pity, but it's almost like a smile of hope or, maybe even friendship.* She takes a deep breath, swallows hard, and opens her mouth. "Can you help me?" she asks the lady. She swallows hard again and clears her throat, "You see, my foot is stuck, and I cannot get free." The lady looks around her.

She throws Senora a water bottle. "Here, take this. You must be tired and thirsty. Drink." Senora gratefully takes a small drink of water. As the water flows down her parched throat, she breathes a sigh of relief.

"Thank you," Senora whispers. The lady grabs one end of a vine and throws it over a branch that is directly above Senora's head.

"Now pour water over your foot and grab onto the vine above you," the lady says. Senora is confused, but she follows the lady's instructions. She pours out the water around her stuck foot, tosses the empty water bottle back at the lady's feet, and reaches up to grab the vine. The lady grabs the other end and begins to pull.

At first, nothing happens except for Senora's body aching as it is getting stretched. Through the pain and the hope rises within her heart, the lady says, "You will know the truth, and the truth will set you free.[10]" Senora feels the mud's grip on her foot loosen as the lady continues to pull. "Your hand shall lead me; your right hand shall hold me,[11]" the lady says.

"I will never give up." Senora's foot comes free, and the lady pulls her to safety. "Thank you," Senora gasps to the lady. "Thank you for helping me." They lie side by side, breathing heavily, trying to catch their breath.

The lady suddenly sits up, pulls out a clean cloth and another water bottle from Senora's backpack. She cleans off Senora's feet, hands, and face. She helps Senora take off her own backpack and finds clean clothes for her. "You're lucky that it was only your foot that was stuck." She points at the mud where Senora had been. "Some people completely disappear in there. He must be protecting you. You must have hope, strong in you. I have seen many others get stuck, but they soon lose their hope and the mud takes over. Hopelessness gives it power and strength."

"Wait! You mean it's alive?" Senora asks.

"Not alive, per se, but it has power."

Senora can see one small tear escape from the lady's eye and slowly fall down her cheek. The lady's shoulders slump a little as she tells Senora the story. "You see, hopelessness and discouragement will eat you up inside. When you let it win, soon only the darkness is left. Light is stronger, and darkness will flee when in the presence of light. So you must be strong and not allow the light to be snuffed out."

"Why did you choose to help me?" Senora asks confused.

"Not important, not important." The lady says, "Remember, you need to ask the right question."

"I want to understand how you are different from the others who only laughed at me and refused to help." Senora says.

---

[10] John 8:32
[11] Psalm 139:10

"The one showed mercy. Jesus said to him, 'You go, and do likewise.[12]. But I say to you here, love your enemies, do good to those who hate you, bless those who curse you, pray for those who abuse you,'[13]" The lady says.

"Are we enemies?" Senora asks.

"No, at least I don't think so. But we're called to be merciful and to show unconditional mercy to all."

Confused, Senora ponders what this lady said. "First of all, who do you mean by we? Second, does all mean everyone? Even those who are mean to you?"

She smiles at Senora in such a kind and compassionate way. "When I say we, I mean all of us. You know those who follow the one and only true King. The one who gave up everything in love of His enemies. He gave up His life to save those who didn't even know they were lost. Those blinded by their evil desires and wrong doings. Those who lied, manipulated, cheated, and even cursed at Him. He loved them all."

"You mean, even when people said mean things to Him, lied to Him, and hurt Him, He still gave up everything? Out of love for those who didn't love Him back?" Senora shakes her head in disbelief.

"Yes, and even as he was dying, He prayed for their forgiveness and salvation."

"But why would He do that? I don't understand. When someone is mean to me, I just feel like something is wrong with me." Senora feels a wave of guilt and shame wash over her.

The lady places her arm around Senora's shoulder. "It's easy to try to get even and pay someone back for hurting you. That's true, but where does it end? Do you feel any better when you're mean to those who are mean to you?"

---

[12]   Luke 10:36b-37
[13]   Luke 6:27-28

Senora considers this lady's question carefully. "Actually, it usually gets worse. I feel terrible. And soon everyone's hurting. But how else do you protect yourself and keep yourself from getting hurt?"

"Well, that's a wise question, but it's also a question that only you can answer for yourself. He loves you and if you trust Him, He will give you the strength and wisdom to endure and grow through the trials that you face. It's through those hurts that we have a choice to make. Will you choose revenge and hatred, losing your true self? Or will you choose to trust His saving grace and healing power to teach you and make you stronger, learn more of who you can become? The choice is yours."

"What's your name?" Senora curiously asks.

"Not important, your journey must not be delayed." The lady says.

"If we're friends, shouldn't I know your name?" Senora says.

"I'm Samantha, but you can call me Sam," the lady says.

"Thank you so much Sam. My name is Nora. It's nice to meet you." They shake hands. Samantha walks Senora to a small cottage over the hill, where she tells Senora she can change her clothes.

They walk together for a time, laughing and sharing stories. As they come over another hill, a small town appears far off in the valley below. "Thanks for everything, Sam." They hug each other; Samantha turns back toward the path. "Wait. You aren't coming with me?"

"Nora, you already have the tools you need. You're never alone."

"But, Sam, how do I know where to go?" Senora says.

"Remember; follow the way of the Red Dragon. Think, and ask the right questions." Samantha points her finger towards the town. "Make your way to the Hills of Courage, as you go, stay alert and seek the clarity you need. I'll not be far if you need help. I promise, help will come. Remember, friendship is a bond, but family is unbreakable," Samantha says.

Senora waves and smiles, content in knowing she has a new friend. Remembering Samantha's final words, "Friendship is a bond, but family is unbreakable," she turns to face the town. "Jo, I'll never give up. Here goes nothing." She adjusts her backpack and slowly starts her descent of the hill toward the town.

PART 2

The Voice Of Fear

CHAPTER 4

Party of Fellowship

Josiah carefully adjusts his footing, and with every step, the rocks slide loosely beneath his feet. He is trying desperately not to fall. He can clearly navigate his path, and as he is carefully planning out his next few steps, the bush behind him rustles. He turns with a start and his foot slips causing him to fall on his back and slide down the hill.

Trees and stones fly past his vision as he quickly descends over the loose gravel. He tries desperately to dig in his heel to slow his decent but without any luck. He scrapes his elbow and bumps his shoulder as he continues to slide.

When the ground starts to level, he is able to reach out his hand and grab a tree branch. He feels all his muscles scream out in pain as he stops his fall and regains his footing. His knee starts to throb again. He winces in pain as he tries to stand up. Sore and tired, he pushes away the pain and reminds himself, "Never give up." He repeats these simple words over and over as he uses the tree branch to regain his balance. He looks around to try to find his location. Josiah had fallen and slid down the hill so fast that he was now in a thick forest. It was quite cool and dark and he can no longer see the sea of stones. "Now where do I go?" he asks himself.

He remembers what his camp director had taught him about getting lost. If he gets lost in the woods, he will see moss growing on the north side of the trees. He feels the tree for moss. When he finally feels some, he tries to remember what he saw when he was by the Tree of Hope and what direction he saw the stones. *Ok, so if that way is north, then* he thinks and scratches his head. *East! I need to go east.* He turns eastward and limps through the trees.

The trees are so thick the sunlight barely penetrates them. It is quite damp and Josiah shivers. He notices that the trees down here are more needle trees and not too many leafy ones anymore. The ground is spongy with moss, and pine cones crunch beneath his feet. Josiah takes a shivery breath. "He gives strength to the weak and power to the powerless,[14]" he says to himself. He sees a path appear through the trees. Cautiously approaching the path, the tall, bearded man appears. Once again, Josiah is startled by the man's sudden appearance. "You scared me," Josiah says breathlessly.

"Don't be afraid, Jo," the man says. Josiah comes close to the man. The man raises his right hand, a hand that could crush him in a second or hold him safe and stable. "Therefore, lift your drooping hands and strengthen your weak knees, and make straight paths for your feet, so that what is lame may not be put out of joint but rather be healed[15]. Remember these words. They will help you along the way." Josiah, not sure what the man just said, scratches his head curiously. "Enter by the narrow gate. For the gate is wide and the way is easy that leads to destruction, and those who enter by it are many.

---

[14]   Isaiah 40:29
[15]   Hebrews 12:12-13

For the gate is narrow and the way is hard that leads to life, and those who find it are few[16]." Josiah looks up and down the path.

"I don't understand. I don't see any gate at all." Josiah turns back toward the man, but he is gone. He is confused, but he remembers he needs to find his sister. Josiah turns and heads east down the path.

As he walks, the pathway widens, but strangely, the trees seem thicker, and the forest feels damp and dreary. His breath gets heavy, and the air is cold.

The pathway suddenly veers sharply to the left, heading south. Josiah starts to think about the man's words: "'Therefore lift your droopy hands and strengthen your weak knees'[5]." Josiah touches his sore knee, thankful that the bleeding has stopped. "Make straight paths for your feet." He ponders these words. "What do I do now?" he asks himself. "If I am to make straight paths for my feet, and this wide path is turning south, do I continue to follow it?" Josiah looks around, feeling lost. "Show me the way," he whispers.

He looks ahead and sees what might have been a path at one time. *The way is hard that leads to life, and those who find it are few[6].* Josiah remembers. He thinks to himself, *if I continue on the larger path, my path will no longer be straight. If I take what looks like a path, it will be hard, but it will probably lead me to life.* Josiah looks back and forth between the larger path and the smaller one.

Josiah is unsure which path to choose, so he sits down to think. As he considers his options, a young lady approaches him. Her eyes are emerald green; her hair flows freely past her shoulders and looks as though it is sunlight itself. She is tall, slender, and almost floats as she approaches him. She stops right in front of Josiah, asking, "Are you alright?" Her voice

---

[16]   Matthew 7:13-14

is as gentle as a light breeze. "You seem sad. What's wrong?" Her voice is still soft and almost hypnotizing.

Josiah says, "My sister is missing, I'm on a journey to find her."

"Ok, so what's the problem?" the lady asks, with a twinkle in her eyes and a strange smile forming, she poses another question: "Is your sister strong?" Josiah thinks about this lady's odd question.

"Yes, she's strong and quite stubborn, if that's what you mean." Josiah thinks some more.

"Well, if she's strong she should be able to save herself, right?" the lady asks and continues without waiting for a response. "What's your name?"

"I'm Josiah," he replies.

"Nice to meet you. I'm Scarlett. Hey, I know what would cheer you up, Jo. Can I call you Jo?"

"Sure, I guess." Josiah shrugs.

"Come with me. I'm going to the Phantasm Oasis. It's really fun. We dance, have lots of laughs, and we play lots of board games. Do you want to come?" Josiah loves board games and playing with friends. He jumps to his feet with great excitement, and he's overwhelmed with the thought that such a pretty, kind young lady would invite him to this gathering place. He's so lost in his joy and excitement that he almost forgets about Senora.

Josiah looks briefly at the small path and Scarlett puts her hand on his shoulder. "Come with me." Her voice sings in his ear, and suddenly he feels dizzy. Scarlett takes his hand and helps turn him around. "Come with me, Jo. You must be tired from your long journey. Come." Josiah starts to follow Scarlett southward down the path. He feels like he's in a dream.

Josiah agrees to go. "But only for a little while. I'll only play one game. Agreed?"

Scarlett smiles sweetly. "Great! Let's go, it's only just around the bend." She leads him through a misty fog, and Josiah sees a glow in the sky. The trees quickly thin, and his eyes widen at the site of the largest, most elegant house he has ever seen. Other kids around his age laugh and joke with one another. All around him, music plays and kids laugh. She leads him up a small flight of stairs and through the front door.

A group of kids stand at the door when she and Josiah walk up the stairs. Scarlett lets go of Josiah's hand and hugs each one as they welcome them. They enter the house, and Josiah stumbles slightly, sending a shiver down his spine. He feels heavy and dizzy as the room comes into focus; the entry is large with a bright crystal chandelier hanging from a large archway ceiling. The marble floor is as white as diamonds, and the walls are bright red. The music is so loud that Josiah covers his ears to drawn out the noise. He doesn't recognize the songs playing, but keeps an open mind.

To his right, several kids play a card game he's never seen played. Scarlett pulls him farther into the crowd. "This way, Jo. I know the perfect game for you." The room seems to be spinning as he's pulled through a sea of faces.

Scarlett stops suddenly, and Josiah almost bumps into her back. "Hey, everyone." Scarlett raises her hands in the air, and the whole room falls silent. "This is Jo. Make him feel welcome."

Scarlett disappears in the crowd of dancing children. The first group Josiah had seen at the door enters behind him. One of the boys places his hand on Josiah, and a shiver chills him to his bones. "Welcome, Jo. I'm Spitts." The boy holds out his hand to shake Josiah's, his voice sounding mellow yet raspy. When Josiah turns to inspect the room, he suddenly finds himself facing a thin, pale-faced boy with dull gray eyes. Josiah opens his mouth to ask if he is not feeling well, but before he can say anything, Scarlett returns, laughing.

She grabs Josiah's arm and whispers in his ear, "I found a game of Risk. Do you want to play?" Josiah forgets about this boy with extreme pale complexion and quickly agrees because

Risk is his favourite game. She leads him through the crowd of dancing children to a group of eight gathered on the floor in the corner. "I found a new player," she says. The group turns to look up at Josiah and motions for him to join them.

Scarlett takes Josiah by the shoulders and sits him down. Josiah is excited to feel so welcomed and accepted. He looks into their eyes and another shiver runs down his spine. Everyone has the same dull, gray eyes. They're thin and pale too. One of the kids holds out his hand, saying, "John's the name. Over there is Peter, Jake, Sylvia, Jordan, Isaac, Tiffany, and Chris." When Josiah touches John's hand, he only feels cold. Fear starts to well up within him. He does want to belong, and he does want to play Risk, but a small question runs through his mind. *Why are they all so thin, pale, and cold?*

Scarlett shakes him out of his own thoughts. "Well, are you going to play?" His head starts to spin as if he's in a fog.

"Maybe, just one game," Josiah says reluctantly. Scarlett's smile is peculiar as she hands him the dice.

"Place your men," she says. Josiah looks down at the board, and it looks much larger than he has ever seen. The game board has many different places and countries that he has never seen or heard of before. As he places his first player, the hair on the back of his neck stands up, making him shiver.

"Josiah?" His name echoes in his mind from the gentle, familiar voice of the tall, bearded man. Josiah jumps at the sound of his own name. On the other side of the room, the tall bearded man appears again.

Scarlett laughs in his ear and Josiah begins to forget who this man is. He places another player on the board. "Josiah." Josiah shivers, and he looks around at the other kids in the room. They laugh and joke with each other, but they stare blankly as if they are in a trance. Scarlett appears differently to him, and she doesn't seem to notice the empty looks on her friend's faces. Josiah turns and looks at her again. Her hair is shining even brighter than before. He sees the man again, this time, a little closer to him.

"Remember your journey. Remember. Josiah. Make straight your paths. Remember," the man's words scream in Josiah's ears. Startled, he looks around at the kids again. They all still seem as if they are in a trance, but Josiah cannot be sure who is enchanting them.

"What do I need to remember? Why am I the only one who hears you?" Josiah yells.

The man moves closer to the door. "Josiah, do not give into the temptations. Your strength can prevail. You only have to want to."

Scarlett smirks. "Who are you talking to? Relax. Have fun. That's what's important."

She places a set of dice in his hands. "Play, Jo. It's your turn." Josiah is confused, and he feels as if his head is in the same fog Scarlett had lead him through when they entered this house. "Play," she whispers in his ear and pats his shoulder. Josiah rolls the dice, and John rolls three more. There is a large flash of light, and he can see John almost fall over. "Jo wins this fight." Scarlett places the dice back in his hands. As the smoke clears, John sits up into position once again. He looks much paler than before.

Scarlett whispers in Josiah's ear again. "Come on, Jo. It's your roll." Josiah rolls the dice again. There's another flash of light, and Josiah is blinded briefly. Out of the corner of his eye, he can see Sylvia fall to her side. "Good. You win again." Scarlett pats Josiah on the shoulder and moves toward Sylvia, who he had seen fall. He watches as Scarlett lifts Sylvia to her feet. Scarlett sparkles, and she smiles over her shoulder at Josiah. Sylvia looks very weak and pale. He looks around the room and begins to see the others, all pale in comparison to Scarlett.

Some of the children laugh, and their faces seem far off, almost lost in a dream, lifeless. He catches a glimpse of the man standing at the door.

"Josiah, you must remember what's important."

"Important? What do you mean?" Josiah's mind spins, and he falls against the wall to catch himself.

"Remember, Josiah, you must not forget your journey," The man says to Josiah again.

"My journey?"

"Journey? No, there is no journey. Only fun! Go on, Jo. Place another player on the board, the others are waiting their turn to play." Scarlett's voice sings in his ear.

"Josiah. Remember Senora," the man says.

"Senora?" Josiah asks.

"Who's Senora?" Scarlett laughs again. "Except someone who fights with you. You don't need that. You deserve respect and fun. Go on, place another player. I know that you want to." Scarlett chuckles.

"Senora? Who's Senora?" He shivers.

"Remember. I said, 'Let me remember my song in the night; let me meditate in my heart.' Then, my spirit made a diligent search.[17]" He hears the man's voice again. Josiah's eyes start to pan the crowd, and he can see the man in the hallway. "But you take courage. Do not let your hands be weak, for your work shall be rewarded.[18] And he said, 'O man greatly loved, fear not, peace be with you; be strong and of good courage.'[19]" The man's voice fades away.

Josiah feels as if his energy and breath are failing him. He drops the dice out of his hands and slowly manages to reach a crawl. He feels heavy; "Therefore lift your droopy hands and strengthen your weak knees and make straight paths for your

[17] Psalm 77:6
[18] 2 Chronicles 15:7
[19] Daniel 10:19a

feet." The man's words are as a faint whisper in his ears. The ground beneath Josiah shakes. He looks around, but no one seems to notice. He forces himself to stand, and he feels like cement is weighing him down. He feels dizzy and breathless.

The children laugh some more, and some boys start to wrestle in the corner of the room. John runs over to cheer them on. "Come on, Zach. You can beat Weldon."

Scarlett walks up to Weldon, who is on the bottom. She bends down and touches Weldon's cheek. Josiah notices Weldon go limp, and Zach jumps. Other children cheer as Zach stands. "You win," Scarlett says. Her hair is shining like sunshine, and the glow of fire and warmth calls to draw people in. Her contagious laughter is like a magnet, pulling you in, poisoning the brain.

Josiah desperately looks around the room. "I have to get out of here." He tries to push his way through the thick crowd, distancing himself from Scarlett and the Risk game. Madly searching for a way out, he sees the man again walking out of the room. Josiah pushes his way through and makes his way out of the room. He looks around to find the man, and then he catches a glimpse of him standing by a nearby window.

Josiah starts to push his way through the crowd toward him; soon, he feels a hand on his shoulder. He turns around to see Scarlett smiling at him. Josiah's head starts to spin again. "Jo, do you not like that game?"

"I did, but I need to get going."

"Going where?"

"I was looking for…"

"What? What were you looking for?"

"I…I…" Josiah feels a headache coming on as he rubs his forehead, trying desperately to remember.

Scarlett smiles at Josiah. "Come. Jo. I can help you."

"Yes. That's right. I was trying to find something."

"You were looking for your home, Jo."

Josiah shakes his head, feeling dizzy and confused. *Home? Was that what I was looking for?* He questions his own thoughts.

"Jo, you are home. Look around you. All of these friends. We are your family." Scarlett smiles at him again. Josiah turns his head and looks around at the sea of faces. He sees the window. *You're home.* He can hear the words play in his own head. His vision blurs, and he shakes his head to adjust. He sees the man again. Suddenly, he remembers.

"Stop. Not my home. Nora? I was looking for Nora." His voice is merely a whisper. He pulls away from Scarlett's touch.

Scarlett laughs again, distracting Josiah from his own thoughts. He pushes her away, and says, "*No.* Nora is my sister. She needs me, and I need her. I will help her, and you will not distract me from my journey any longer. Excuse me." Josiah starts to push his way through the crowd toward the door. He thinks it is impossible for him to get to the door because the crowd is so large, and he feels boxed in. Suddenly, he feels a warm hand reach out through the crowd take hold of his hand and pull him through the crowd. He bursts through the front door, jumps down the stairs, and pushes through the misty fog.

When he looks up, he sees the man holding his hand. The man smiles and gently says, "Never give up. The way to life will be hard but never give up." Josiah hugs the man to thank him. "Remember your journey," the man says. "He gives power to the faint, and to him who has no might, He increases strength.[20]" He turns his head to look up at the man again, but he finds himself alone.

Echoes of children laughing still ring in his ears, beads of sweat drips off his forehead, and he reminds himself: *Never give up. The way to life will be hard, but never give up.* Josiah runs northward down the trail until he stumbles at the bend

---

[20]   Isaiah 40:29

in the path. He falls to his knees, gasping for breath. Alone, he finds himself pondering everything that had happened.

"How much time have I lost? I need to find Nora before it's too late." He turns to face the small faded path and sweeps his hand to push away the branches. He takes a step forward and disappears through the trees.

Josiah struggles as he pushes his way through the tree branches, stumbling with every step. He is tired, and his legs ache from both running and from the branches scratching. When he's about to turn around and give up, he pushes through a set of trees and finds a small, hidden grassy area. The sun is shining, and he can feel its warmth on his face. A slight breeze blows as he breathes in the fresh air. He sits down in the tall grass to rest for a while. Josiah hears a voice on the wind. "Come to me, all who labor and are heavy laden, and I will give you rest.[21]" Josiah looks around sleepily, but he doesn't see anyone. He's so tired from his battle for freedom from Scarlett that he lays his head down and drifts off into a peaceful sleep. "I'll never leave you." He hears his voice, and he takes comfort in these words.

---

[21]   Matthew 11:28

CHAPTER 5

Field of Despair

Senora enters the small rustic town where older, rundown buildings line the narrow streets. She can hear a trickling stream run down through the center of the town. People are shouting and rushing about in all different directions, but no one seems to be getting anything done. She navigates her way through the busy crowd, getting bumped into every few steps. Along one of the streets, there's a row of outdoor merchants calling out to people passing by, trying to sell their merchandise. "Get you lizard scale jewelry here." One merchant says.

"You look thirsty for this delicious, hot Dragons breath tea. Guaranteed to warm you deep down to your toes."

"Warm? Warm you say? I have the finest skins you can find. They will warm you and cloak you from harm."

Such strange items to be selling, Senora thinks, as she approaches one of the booths. "Excuse me." The merchant stops calling out, and looks at her in expectation, "can you direct me to the Hills of Courage?" He glares at her, and calls out to another passer-buyer. Nobody seems to hear or even notice her. "Hello?" Senora makes her way through the busy streets, trying desperately to get someone's attention.

She sees that same shaggy-haired man she had seen on the path. He's selling jewelry waving her over. "Do you know the way to the Hills of Courage? Or are you just going to laugh at me again?" Senora asks the man. A strange smile forms on his face. Not one of those smiles that brightens a room. Not one that even went into his eyes. It was more like a smile that looks through someone and sends chills down their spine. Senora shivers as she gets a feeling of cold.

"You are very beautiful and strong too. I told you that you could get yourself out of your own mess. I was right, wasn't I?" the man says. "Do you want this dazzling diamond necklace?" The man lifts a beautiful, sparkling necklace. "And perhaps this gold ring? I will even give you a sparkling crown, if you want."

"What's the catch?" Senora asks, confused. "I don't have any money."

The man smiles. "Money? No, no, you don't understand. You are such a beautiful, strong girl. I will give you these and so much more. Increase your beauty and grant you fame. People will adore you, as I do already." The man turns the necklace so it sparkles in the sunlight. "Such a beautiful, strong lady deserves beautiful things." The man pulls a bundle of cash out of his pocket. "Hence, I will give you money and these beautiful things. You can buy whatever you want. Whatever your heart desires, it can be yours," the man says.

Senora is dazzled by the beautiful jewels and surprised by this man's offer after his cruel nature along the path; this is a welcome change in attitude. She considers this for a while. "You will have friends, fame, and money to go with such beauty," the man says.

Senora thinks about all she has been through so far and how tiring her journey has been, but she also remembers what Samantha told her, "Keep your life free from the love of money, and be content with what you have. For He has said, 'Never will I leave you nor forsake you.'[22]"

"So, what have you decided, beautiful lady?" the man asks.

"No, thanks," Senora says. As she turns to leave, the man grabs her hand. His hand feels cold as ice and sends a shooting chill up her arm. Senora shivers again, trying to pull out of his grasp.

"I offer you everything, and you say no thanks?" The man smirks at her. "You will be mine. Eventually, they're all mine." Senora pulls her hand away and runs down the street.

She's focused. "I need to find the way. I need to find the Hills of Courage." She climbs a steep street. There are houses on either side. As people pass by her, she tries desperately to ask the way, but everyone appears too busy to answer her. As she climbs this street the crowds of people increase and start shoving her out of the way. Senora spins in circles, desperate to get someone's attention. She gets an elbow in her side, another person steps on her toes, and yet another person shoves her to the side, causing her to bump into the side of a house. As she reaches out her hand to tap someone on the shoulder, a black bag goes over her head. Someone picks her up and throws her over their shoulder. She tries to scream, but her voice is muffled by the bag. As she is fighting to get free, she is hit on the head. All goes black.

Senora wakes up in a small room with no windows, and she's tied up to a chair. "Hello? Is anyone there?" The room suddenly fills with light as a door flies open, and someone shines a bright light in her eyes. Senora squints, trying to focus on something, but her eyes only fill with tears.

"Who are you?" a voice asks.

"Senora," she answers, nervously. "Where am I, and why am I here?" Senora asks.

---

22   Hebrews 13:5

"I am asking the questions here! Not you," the voice yells. "Why are you looking for the Hills of Courage?"

"Please. I'm trying to find my brother, Jo."

"The Hills of Courage. Who told you about this?" the voice asks, demanding an answer.

"What? Why? I only know this is the way I'm supposed to go."

The voice yells, "Silence." A water bottle is handed to her. "Drink." Senora takes a small drink. "Now again. Why are you looking for the Hills of Courage?"

Senora's not sure how to answer. She's scared and confused. The light's turned off, and she hears a door open and close. She's alone.

She's questioned about the Hills of Courage for what seemed like days, but she still persists because she really doesn't know what they want. She never sees the person questioning her because of the light shining in her eyes.

On the fourth day of questioning, someone enters. As usual, they turn on the light, but the voice is different. "You must find the treasure."

"What?" Senora weakly asks. "What is this treasure you speak of? I can't even save myself."

"He'll never leave you nor forsake you,[23]" the new voice says. "Find the Greatest Treasure. A friendship is a bond, but family is unbreakable."

"Sam?" The person comes close and hugs Senora. It is Samantha. Samantha unties Senora. "How did you find me?"

"Whispers mainly," Samantha says in a hushed way. She leads Senora to the door. "I will answer all of your questions once you're safe." Samantha opens the door to the room and turns to look at Senora, "Turn off that light," she whispers. Senora turns off the light and walks over to Samantha. The

---

[23] Hebrews 13:5

two girls kneel together as Samantha looks through the door. "All is clear. Let's go." They stand and go out the door.

They find themselves standing in a hallway of a big building. Samantha turns right and heads down the hallway. "This way," she says to Senora. They turn a corner at the end of the hall and walk through another door. Once through Senora sees a staircase. Samantha leads the way up the stairs. They turn, and as they head up a second flight of stairs, they hear the door behind them open and close. Samantha looks over her shoulder at Senora and yells, "Run." The two girls run up the last few steps as they hear someone running up the stairs after them. At the top of the stairs they turn right and go through another set of doors that lead outside. Samantha leads Senora down a hilly path. They turn and crouch down. Senora sees the man who offered her jewelry come out of the building.

"Where are you?" he yells. "I'll find you. You will not defeat me. You will not discover the truth. You will not win. You hear me?" The girls watch as the man goes back into the building.

"Who was that?" Senora asks.

Samantha turns. "That was Lucas. He will stop at nothing to make sure you do not find the treasure."

"What is this treasure?"

"You need to discover this for yourself." Samantha says. "This is why you must find your brother. It's the only way. Family is unbreakable. Never give up. He'll help you."

"Who will help me?" Senora asks.

"He is the Alpha and the Omega. He's the creator of everything."

"Who is He?" Senora asks again.

"He's the everlasting Father, Prince of Peace. The great *I am*" Samantha says. "He'll protect you and give you the strength you need." Samantha turns and looks down the path. "Follow the Red Dragon; it will lead you to the Hills of Courage."

"You're not coming with me?" Senora asks sadly.

"That's not my journey. It's yours. Find Jo. You need each other. Take care." Three men come out of the building and look around. "Now, go. I will lead them away," Samantha whispers. She stands up and yells out, "Hey all. Come get me if you can." She runs away from Senora. The three men chase her. When Senora cannot see them anymore, she turns and looks toward the path she saw Samantha look at earlier and sees the Red Dragon Fly above her and down the path. "The Red Dragon," Senora says, almost breathless. The path is narrow and grassy, and a barb wire fence lines both sides. She walks down the path.

Senora takes one last look over her shoulder before the building is out of sight. "Good luck, Sam. And thanks again." She smiles and keeps walking. As Senora goes over the next few hills, she can hear gunshots and a vehicle's engine revving. She looks over her shoulder, hoping that Samantha is ok. She's horrified when she sees quads coming over the first hill next to the building. Two people ride fast in her direction.

Senora turns and runs as fast as she can. She stumbles and slides a few times going down another hill. Jumping over a large badger hole, she runs up to a barb wire gate. She frantically opens the gate and climbs through. The quads are getting closer. She quickly closes the gate, turns, and runs.

Her chest is heaving as she struggles up the next hill, gasping for breath. The quads stop at the gate. Senora's relieved because now she can gain some distance between them and herself. She sees something moving up ahead of her: a flash of red. She runs up to it and sees a red flag flapping on the ground. As she picks it up, she sees a symbol of the Red Dragon on it. "What does this mean?" She is startled at the sound of an ear-piercing roar. There is some movement through the grass, and a glint of red flashes once more.

"Follow the way of the Red Dragon," Senora says, repeating Samantha's words.

She can hear the quads engines running again. Looking around frantically to find a place to hide, she runs in the direction of the red movement. She falls to the ground in fear as she hears the roar again. *What is that?* she asks in her mind. "It can't truly be a dragon? Can it?"

The quad engines slow down. She barely lifts her head up enough to see the quad turn suddenly and head back towards the gate at full speed. Smoke rises behind them, and sparks of fire lick at their tires.

Senora places her arm over her mouth, her eyes sting as the smoke reaches her. "Run," Samantha yells. She stands to her feet only to have a blast of wind knock her backward, and she falls into a hole. Facing what looks like an entrance to a tunnel, she makes her way into it. It's large and damp, it appears to be an old drainage pipe. She leans on the cold metal side to catch her breath, coughing to clear the smoke from her lungs.

She wonders why those men keep chasing her. *The Hills of Courage are important, but I am not sure why. I've offended them somehow, even though I don't think I have done anything wrong. It must have something to do with the Red Dragon I have heard so much about.* Senora turns to inspect the tunnel she's standing in, it's quite large, and she can easily stand up in it. The edges are damp with cold water, and it is made of corrugated steel. As she inspects the tunnel, she can hear voices coming through the smoke.

She crouches down in the tunnel and squints through the smoke. She sees Lucas and two other men emerge through the smoke.

"She must not have gone far. Find her." Lucas yells at the other two. One man runs to the right while the other runs to the left. Lucas walks toward the dip in the ground and barb wire fence where Senora's hiding. She looks around, wondering what to do. Trembling, she's refuses to give into her own fear.

She swallows hard and holds her breath. *Please don't let them find me,* she thinks. He gets closer and closer to her position. Suddenly, his phone buzzes, and he raises it to his ear. "OK, what do you want to ask me?" Lucas rolls his eyes as he listens. "Kat and Crystal? Why bring them up? I told you, they are gone. We have been over this. Delores is a traitor." He sighs in frustration.

"Look, I am pursuing a new threat. No, my love, I am not changing the subject. All will become clear. You just need to trust me." He pauses to listen to the responses. "Dead end? What do you mean dead end? Stop, just listen." He growls in frustration. "I am pursuing Nora. I told you she will not defeat you. What? You are the most important. But, I am so close. I can feel it. Now? The castle? Fine." Lucas shoves his phone back in his pocket. Senora hears Lucas growl in frustration as he motions for the other two to head back through the smoke towards the building again. Before he turns to leave, he yells "You may have won the first round but believe me, you'll see me again. You may have made your way through the Hills of Courage, but you'll never find the treasure. I'll stop you. You're not strong enough to defeat me." He turns and disappears as the smoke surround him.

Senora questions why they left her there. Why did they not continue to look for her? Who called them back? Senora turns, slowly makes her way through to the other side of the tunnel, and crawls to a nearby barb wire fence. She climbs through to the other side.

She looks ahead, and as far as she can see, is a big open field. There is a leaf covered sign on the ground beside her. As she brushes away the leaves, she reads the sign. *Warning: Now entering the Field of Despair. Enter at your own risk.*

She's so tired from all her running, but she knows the men chasing her could return anytime. She cannot stop now because it's not safe here. *If I step out and try to make it across this field, will those men see me? If they return, and she stays, they'll capture me,* her mind races. She squares her shoulders, stands, and steps out from the cover of the trees.

When she looks out over the endless field again, she notices a thick, white fog rolling in. Senora's both relieved for the covered protection but also afraid of losing her way because it'll be difficult to see. She doesn't have a choice and steps into this strange fog.

Senora can hear the faint, muffled sound of quads returning to her previous location. Fear takes over, and she runs farther into the fog. She can no longer see where she is or hear anything. The air is damp, and she shivers.

"Nora, Nora," A familiar voice says. She thinks that she is hearing things and slows her pace to a steady walk. "Nora," the voice says again.

"Nora? Is that you?" Senora remembers. She laughs when she remembers skipping rocks at the lake and climbing trees with Trevor.

"Trevor?" She hears a different voice calling out her brother's name. This voice reminds her of Robert. "Trevor, let's build a fort together," she hears Robert say, "but Nora cannot help." Senora remembers well. "Come on, Trevor, you're such a great builder. Nora can't build. She's too young. She'll find other friends to play with." Senora sees Robert motioning to Trevor to come with him. "She'll be fine," Robert says, "she doesn't need to know about this."

"Trevor, Trevor," she calls out again. "Where are you?" Senora can faintly see what looks like Trevor standing a short distance from her. She wants to run to him and give him a big hug, but her feet don't seem to want to move.

"Trevor," Robert yells. She's startled to hear his voice behind her. Robert puts his hand on Trevor's shoulder. "Come on, Trevor. The building awaits. It'll be an amazing fort. Just imagine the structure. We can even add a pool, if you want." Trevor smiles at Robert and sadly looks toward Senora. "Come on, Trevor. You want to do cool stuff, don't you?"

Senora remembers her longing to spend time with Trevor. "I miss you so much," she whispers. The fog lifts a little to reveal a memory, a time she had long since forgotten. She sees herself digging in the sand on the coastal shore. Josiah is jumping the small waves as they ripple over the sand. "I betcha I can jump higher," she teases Josiah.

"I doubt that," Josiah scoffs. She drops her shovel, runs at the next incoming wave, and jumps.

"Big deal. That was just a small one. Watch this." Josiah runs waste deep into the ocean water. He turns and grins at Senora as she sees a huge wave emerge from behind Josiah. "Jo, Look out." she yells. She feels the wind rush past her as her dad runs into the ocean like a flash and dives in as Josiah disappears under the weight of the water. She blinks through tears as she sees her dad surface without Josiah. "Where is he, Dad?" Her words seem to hang in the air as Trevor jumps in after her dad. The two disappear into the water together. "1, 2, 3," she starts to count the length of time they are out of sight. Soon, they re-emerge, pulling Josiah back onto the shore. The fog falls in around her again, and she shivers once more, feeling the weight and pain of this memory.

The fog reveals another scene: Robert and two other girls approach her. "Four eyes, four eyes. You're a four eyes." "Bean pole, bean pole." "You're so stupid. Nobody wants you around," one of the girls says, and Senora looks down at the ground.

She sees Robert next to Trevor again. "Come on, Trevor. Let's go build." She sees the other girl put something in Robert's hand. "Go on; see how far you can throw it." Robert looks in his hand and sees a rock. "Come on. It won't hurt anything." Robert tosses the rock. Senora feels the pain as the rock brushes against her cheek. The girl hands him another. "Fun, isn't it?" Robert throws again. "Come on, Robert. You're doing great. Throw another," the girl says to encourage him. Senora feels another rock hit her knee and one hit her arm. She staggers in pain, but then she notices the fog lighten a little. She sees the shock of fear and regret on Robert's face as blood streams down her arm. "Go on, Robert, you're doing great. Throw another." The girl hands Robert another rock. She's laughing. Senora's eye well up with tears of sorrow.

Senora looks up with tears in her eyes. "I thought we were friends." The rock falls out of Robert's hand.

"Run, you big baby," someone says. She looks around her to see Robert laughing.

The fog thickens again, and Senora finds herself alone. The pain of the rocks are gone. She wraps her arms around herself and cries. She can hear another voice, one she doesn't recognize. "But God, being rich in mercy, because of the great love with which he loved us, even when we were dead in our trespasses, made us alive together with Christ by grace you have been saved and raised up with him in the heavenly places in Christ Jesus, so that in the coming ages He might show the immeasurable riches of his grace in kindness towards us in Christ Jesus. For by grace you have been saved through faith. And this is not your own doing; it is the gift of God.[24]" Senora listens closely but she's confused and she doesn't understand what this voice is telling her.

"But God showed His love for us in that while we were still sinners, Christ died for us.[25]" The voice says. Its words are spoken with gentleness and pure love. "My heart becomes not within me. As I mused, the fire burned; then I spoke with my tongue: 'O Lord, make me know my end and what is the measure of my days; let me know how fleeting I am.[26]" Senora considers these words carefully. She can hear Robert again. "Nora?" He hands her a box.

"What's this?" she asks.

---

[24] Ephesians 2:4-9
[25] Romans 5:8
[26] Psalm 39:1

"Just open it. It's a gift." Robert smiles devilishly. She opens the box slowly and pulls out a nice skipping rope. "I knew that you wanted one." She sees Robert's expression changes drastically, and he starts to laugh. She looks down at her hands and sees that she is holding a snake. She throws it away. The fog thickens again.

"We are hard pressed on every side, but not crushed; perplexed, but not in despair; persecuted, but not abandoned; struck down, but not destroyed.[27] Do not be conformed to the pattern of this world but be transformed by the renewing of your mind. Then you will be able to test and approve what His will is His good, pleasing, and perfect will.[28] The righteous person may have many troubles, but the Lord delivers him from them all,[29]" the voice says.

Senora covers her ears with her hands and closes her eyes. She tries desperately not to remember those painful memories. The weight of the fog feels heavier than ever. Her head is spinning, and she tries to block out this unknown voice and the pain of these memories. Her ears seem filled with the sound of the taunts of her peers, and Robert's jeers. Senora falls to her knees; her eyes begin to sting as the tears start to form.

"Truthful lips endure forever, but a lying tongue is but for a moment. Deceit is in the heart of those who devise evil, but those who plan peace have joy.[30] They bend their tongue like a bow; falsehood and not truth has grown strong in the land, for they proceed from evil to evil, and they do not know me, declares the Lord.[31]"

"Who are you? Can you help me?" Senora asks the unfamiliar voice. She hears Robert laughing off in the distance.

---

[27]   2 Corinthians 4:8-9
[28]   Romans 12:2
[29]   Psalm 24:19
[30]   Proverbs 12:19-20
[31]   Jeremiah 9:31

"You will keep in perfect peace those whose minds are steadfast, because they trust in you. Trust in the Lord forever, for the Lord, the Lord himself, is the Rock eternal.[32] We also rejoice in God through our Lord Jesus Christ. We have now received this reconciliation through Him. Therefore, just as sin entered the world through one man, and death through sin, in this way death spread to all men, because all sinned.[33] For He chose us in Him before the creation of the world to be holy and blameless in His sight. In love He predestined us for adoption to son ship through Jesus Christ, in accordance with His pleasure and will- to the praise of His glorious grace, which He has freely given us in the One He loves.[34]"

"I surrender to your loving arms. Help me find your love and rest in your peace," she says, sending a prayer to God. "I need you." She buries her face in her hands.

"See, I have engraved you on the palms of my hands; your walls are ever before me.[35] For we are God's workmanship, created in Christ Jesus to do good works, which God prepared in advance for us to do.[36]"

"Thank you, Father, for loving me and showing me my value. In Jesus name, amen."

Senora sees Robert standing with Trevor. "Hey there, Trevor. Want to see something cool?"

"Hey Bobbie, whatcha talkin' bout?"

"Come to my house. My dad has such a cool collection. You'll love it."

Senora staggers to her feet and tries desperately to scream 'no,' but her voice is caught in her throat.

---

[32]   Isaiah 26:3-4
[33]   Romans 5:11-12
[34]   Ephesians 1:4-6
[35]   Isaiah 49:16
[36]   Ephesians 2:10

She sees Robert pull out a long rifle, and he hands it to Trevor. She sees as Trevor spins it around and inspects it. "You're right, Bobbie. This is a neat collection."

Senora hears yelling from somewhere as she sees Robert slump his shoulders.

"Here. Don't worry about it, Bobbie."

"You don't have to live with it every day. Trevor, they're always fighting."

"Hang in there. Life will get better."

"How can you be so sure?" Robert looks up at Trevor. Trevor hands the rifle back to Robert.

Senora feels a lump forming in her throat. She has never seen this before. How can she be seeing it now? All the other things she has seen have been memories, but this one is different. She fearfully stares on, paralyzed and confused, but not willing to look away. "I need to know what really happened that day. I need to understand."

The voices of yelling increase and Senora can see the turmoil in Robert's eyes and the concern in Trevor's. "I will stay with you, if you want."

Senora staggers to her feet now, trying to run to Trevor, but no matter how hard or fast she runs she doesn't seem to get any closer.

"No. I'll be fine. You just go. No one else needs to endure this." Robert closes the gun safe and walks up the stairs. Senora now hears Robert yelling at his dad. She sees Trevor looking around in desperation. She sees Robert stumble down the stairs. Trevor runs to him as Robert screams out in pain. "Bobbie, are you alright?" Panic takes over as she sees Robert's dad step down the stairs. "Stop this madness," Trevor shouts.

"Mind your own business, boy. This is between me and my son." Senora sees Robert's dad kick Trevor off balance. Trevor stumbles back as Robert's dad starts kicking Robert several times. "You worthless piece of skin. Why don't you just grow up? Your mom understands her place. I need you to understand yours."

Senora falls in desperation, and now she understands the pain Robert carries. "Stop," Trevor screams. Robert's dad turns and walks over to Trevor. "I said," He says as he kicks Trevor in the stomach, "mind your own business." Robert stumbles to the gun safe, reaches in, and grabs a small black handgun.

"Dad, stop hurting my friend," Robert whispers. Senora sees Robert's dad reach down and pick Trevor up off the ground.

"Boy, you need to learn a lesson." He turns to face Robert. "You're not man enough to stand up to me." He steps forward, using Trevor as a human shield. Senora sees beads of sweat trickle down Robert's face. His dad steps closer.

Senora falls to her knees, and the tears flow freely down her cheeks as she hears Robert, "Please, Dad. Let him go. Stop this madness. You need help."

She sees Robert's mom run down the stairs. Robert turns to look toward her as his dad throws Trevor towards Robert. She hears the gun go off. "This is all on you, boy," Robert's dad says.

"Get out," Robert's mom yells. Senora hears Robert's dad laugh and walk back up the stair.

Robert grabs the phone and calls 911. Robert's mom reaches for her cell phone and starts calling Senora's house number. Then, the memory fades away. Senora slumps forward and cries. "All this time, I've blamed Robert. Trevor was only trying to help him. Please forgive me. Take away this hate and heal my heart," Senora screams out in desperation.

"See what kind of love the Father has given to us that we should be called children of God; and so we are. The reason why the world does not know us is that it did not know him. Beloved, we are God's children now, and what we will be has not yet appeared; but we know that when he appears we shall be like him, because we shall see him as he is.[37]"

---

[37] 1 John 3:1-2

"Therefore God has highly exalted Him and bestowed on Him the name that is above every name, so that at the name of Jesus every knee should bow, in heaven and on earth and under the earth, and every tongue confess that Jesus Christ is Lord, to the glory of God the Father.[38]"

"You are loved and while you hated Him, He died for you," the voice whispers in her ears. "You are not worthless. You are a masterpiece."

Senora finally understands Jesus. Jesus is God's son, and He created her. He doesn't make worthless things. He creates masterpieces. A love overpowers and engulfs her; life would never be the same. With a lump in Senora's throat, she falls to her knees again. "God, if you can hear me, help me believe. Change my heart, renew my hope, enter my heart, and forgive me. Lord Jesus, I need you. I'm sorry for not thinking of others. Can you ever forgive me? Please, I cannot do this on my own."

"Are not five sparrows sold for two pennies? And not one of them is forgotten before God. Why, even the hairs on your head are all numbered. Fear not, you are of more value than many sparrows.[39]" Senora begins to understand how valuable her life really is.

"God, forgive me and teach me my value," Senora prays.

"For this is my blood of the covenant, which is poured out for many for the forgiveness of sins.[40] Put on then, as God's chosen ones, holy and beloved, compassionate hearts, kindness, humility, meekness, and patience, bearing with one another and, if one has a complaint against another, forgiven each other; as the Lord has forgiven you, so you also must

---

[38]   Philippians 2:4-11
[39]   Luke 12:6-7
[40]   Matthew 26:28

forgive. And above all these you must put on love, which binds everything together in perfect harmony.[41]

A wave of peace washes over Senora, and she rises to her feet. She takes a few steps forward. "In Him we have redemption through His blood, the forgiveness of our trespasses, according to the riches of His grace, which he lavished upon us in all wisdom and insight making known to us the mystery of His will, according to His purpose, which He set forth in Christ as a plan for the fullness of time, to unite all things in Him, things in heaven and things on earth.[42] For you formed my inward parts; you knit me together in my mother's womb. I praise you, for I am fearfully and wonderfully made. Wonderful are your works; my soul knows it very well. My frame was not hidden from you, when I was being made in secret intricately woven in the depths of the earth.[43]"

With every new step she takes through this misty fog, the sound of Robert's laughter fades off and is finally silenced.

"Thank You for lavishing Your grace on me." Senora feels both her courage and strength build. She continues to walk through the mist and notices the fog lifting.

She shivers as a new memory comes into focus "Come on dad, can't we stay out a little longer?" Senora says.

"The fish are not biting today. Besides mom should have supper just about ready back at the campsite. She will not want us to be late. You know how she feels about having a cold supper." Dad says.

Senora watches on with anger boiling up within her. "Well, ok. But can we go out fishing after supper again?"

"Sure, that should work out good. I promise we will go out after supper." Dad says as he turns the boat towards shore.

---

[41] Colossians 3:12-14
[42] Ephesians 1:7-10
[43] Psalm 139:13-15

Senora's anger builds, "Only broken promises." She whispers to herself and she rolls her eyes.

She kneels down to take in the scene. "one, two.....ten.... fifteen..." Senora finds herself growling and grumbling to herself. "Dad, you said after supper we could go back out to fish some more."

"Sure things." Her Dad says as he slurps down his sixteenth beer.

"No you will not." Mom speaks up. "You're drunk, and I will not allow you to take the boat out with Nora in this state."

"But he promised me." Senora says as she sees Dad fall off his chair and sleep on the ground. Senora hugs her knees to her chest. "Why show me this. Dad always breaks his promises to me. It feels like he doesn't even care."

"Please forgive the trespass of your servant. For the Lord will certainly make my lord a sure house, because my lord is fighting the battles of the Lord, and evil shall not be found in you so long as you live.[44]

"Why should I forgive him? He broke his promise. His beer was more important than me." Senora says.

"Blessed is the one whose transgression is forgiven, whose sin is covered.[45]" The voice says.

"Yes, but all he thinks about is himself. He wouldn't even come home for Trevor's funeral." Senora says.

The fog pushes in on her, making it hard to breath.

She can faintly hear the buttons being pushed on a phone and ring tones. "Hello? Dad, Are you coming home soon? You know Trevor's funeral is tomorrow." Senora can hear her own words hang in the air.

"Huh, what? Nora? Is that you? Yeah, I'll be there. I promise. Nothing will keep me away." Dad says.

---

[44] 1 Samuel 25:28
[45] Psalm 32:1

"But he never came. On one of the most important family days, a time to be together, as a family. He promised. But once again, he broke that promise. He abandoned us. What was so important? That he didn't come?" Senora says.

Faintly she can see her dad sitting on the floor of a hotel room with a case of beer beside him.

"Here's to you Trevor. At least you no longer have to be burdened with the stresses of life." Senora looks on as she sees Dad drink down another can of beer. "What kind of father am I, I couldn't save you. Jo and Nora are probably better off without me. I certainly know Karen will be happier if I'm not around." He takes another drink. Senora watches on as she sees her dad pick up his phone. "Hello?"

"Frank, are you drunk again? How could you? Today of all days, on Trevor's funeral no less." Senora hears her mom's voice on the phone. She watches on as Dad throws the phone across the room and smashes it against the wall.

"Everyone would be better off." He takes another drink and the scene fades away.

"For if you forgive others their trespasses, your heavenly Father will also forgive you, but if you do not forgive their trespasses, neither will your Father forgive your trespasses.[46]

"I never knew the darkness and bitterness he carried with him." Senora says.

"Blessed are those whose lawless deeds are forgiven, and whose sins are covered; blessed is the man against whom the Lord will not count his sins.[47]"

"He is just so caught up in his own anger to care that the rest of us are hurting too." Senora says.

Senora is startled out of her thoughts when she hears Trevor's voice. "No, Nora. Love is everything. You need to

[46] Matt. 6:14-15
[47] Romans 4:7-8

forgive Dad, Bobbie, Bobbie's parents. Allow your heart to heal. He does love you, but sometimes parents lose focus. We cannot control how others act or what they say, but we can control who we are, how we act, and what we say."

"You are precious. You are loved. You're forgiven. Will you choose to forgive?" Trevor whispers in her ear.

Senora can no longer contain the tears as they fall freely down her cheeks. "I do forgive. Help me, God, to heal and love," she prays.

"Where there is forgiveness of these, there is no longer any offering for sin. Therefore, brothers, since we have confidence to enter the holy places by the blood of Jesus, by the new and living way He opened for us through the curtain, that is, through His flesh, and since we have a great priest over the house of God, let us draw near with a true heart in full assurance of faith, with our hearts sprinkled clean from an evil conscience and our bodies washed with pure water.[48]"

Something starts to appear in the fog. "Let us hold fast the confession of our hope without wavering, for He who promised is faithful." She runs toward whatever she's seeing. As she reaches what looks like a bridge over a slow-moving river, her heart fills with anticipation and hope.

"Thank you, Jesus. May You give me forgiveness and wisdom." Once she touches the bridge, the fog melts away, and the sun shines warmly upon her.

"Nora, there is peace in forgiveness. Remember you're not alone." Trevor's voice melts away with the fog. She climbs down the hill and kneels under the bridge to rest. Her muscles are in pain, and she pants for breath. When she notices her cheeks drenched with tears, she wipes them away, and she closes her eyes. She's so tired and exhausted that sleep takes over.

---

[48] Hebrew 10:18-22

CHAPTER 6

The Stone Maze of Knowledge

Josiah stretches, yawns, and rubs his eyes. *I had such a strange dream,* he thinks to himself. Then, he hears an eagle call. He opens his eyes, "Aww, it was not a dream," he says as his head and shoulders droop. The eagle calls again, and he looks up into the sky. Squinting and groaning, he says, "Ok, I'm up. Now I need to find that Maze of Knowledge," he gives himself a pep talk. He slowly and painfully stands up, dusts off his clothes, and inspects his surroundings. Josiah sees the small path that he walked on yesterday, but it seems to have stopped in this small grove. He spins around in circles, taking in everything.

A few trees lean on each other, creating an archway. He runs over to inspect it, kicks some leaves around, and notices the same type of thin, untraveled trail like the one he took yesterday. He's still not able to see anything but trees. His heart fills with hope.

Josiah pushed his way through when he hears a fierce growl. He looks and sees something moving behind him. The growl grows louder. Out of fear and without even thinking, Josiah turns and runs down the path. He can hear tree branches breaking behind him. Whatever it is, it's moving fast. Josiah jumps into a nearby bush and waits. The thing that is chasing him is getting closer. "Maybe it won't see me and it will just pass by." Josiah tries to calm himself. He subconsciously slows his breathing.

Josiah feels the ground shake as each step gets closer. The dry, brown leaves crackle, and Josiah closes his eyes. He can feel the wind blow on his face. His heart feels as if it is beating in his throat, and he tries desperately to swallow. The growl is almost deafening. Josiah covers his ears with his hands and curls his knees up to his chest. He feels a warm breath over him. Holding his breath, his mind starts to spin. He wants to run and scream, but he is paralyzed with fear. As he sits there too petrified to move or even open his eyes, he remembers a verse his camp director used to tell him when he was scared. Josiah whispers, "The Lord is my shepherd, I shall not fear. He makes me lie down in green pastures. He leads me by still waters.[49]"The growling turns to screaming as if the beast is in pain. "He restores my soul. He leads me in paths of righteousness for His name sake.[50]"

The beast jumps around and runs away from Josiah. "Even though I walk through the valley of the shadow of death, I will fear no evil, for you are with me; your rod and your staff, they comfort me.[51]" Josiah now realizes that the only sound he hears is his own voice yelling out this verse. The beast is gone! He slowly opens his eyes and sees that he is alone and the bush he was in is gone. He's lying in the middle of the

---

[49]   Psalm 23:1-2
[50]   Psalm 23:3
[51]   Psalm 23:4

path. He stands a little shaken but at peace. "Thank you, God," Josiah says.

Josiah jumps at the sound of the beast's growl. He forces himself to turn in the direction of the sound, but he only sees a small flash of silver as the beast flies through a cloud and out of sight. "What was that?" Josiah asks himself. He swallows hard and tries to regain some control. "Ok, Josiah. You need to keep going. Fear cannot paralyze you," he says to reassure himself. He turns and continues to walk down the path. Josiah senses pain when he tries to bend his elbow. He looks down at it and notices it's bleeding, and a little bit of blood is dripping off his hand. The arm of his coat appears to be torn and is red with blood. He pulls off his coat and drops it on the path. Remembering his bandana in his coat pocket, he bends to retrieve it. Using his good arm, he dabs his elbow and then ties his bandana around his arm with his good hand and teeth.

Josiah is relieved that this beast is gone, but he wonders if he will see it again. He shivers at the thought. He's unsure why it left but he's grateful. Once his wound starts to feel better, Josiah throws his coat off the path into the tall grass and continues. He kicks some leaves around at his feet, and the breeze blows by his ear. Pushing through the last set of trees, he sees the path continue over a field and up a hill again. He brushes off his clothes and continues on his journey.

Startled to hear branches breaking behind him, he turns to see a small shadow retreat back into the trees. He's safe, for now. He slowly walks out from the cover of the tree branches, nervously because he fears the beast's return. Unsure of the origin of the beast, he begins to question whether he is safe or not. The questions run in and out of his mind. He stops in his own tracks. He listens, but he notices that he doesn't hear anything. Normally, this would be a relief, but this time, no peace came with this silence. No birds were singing, no wind blowing, not even gophers chattering. Suddenly, he can hear some branches breaking behind him. He looks desperately to find a place to hide. "God, please show me what to do," he prays quietly.

He sees a small hole in the ground about three feet from where he's standing. It's probably only three feet deep and about two feet wide. Josiah could barely fit in. He shuffles his feet as he inches closer to this hole. He steps down into it and realizes it is only waist deep. He kneels and leans his head down. Anyone walking by would not be able to even notice him. The ground shakes with every step of something moving closer. He shivers when he feels some dirt fall in on him and trickle down the back of his neck. His blood goes cold as if someone was breathing down on him.

"You're nothing. You're weak. He cannot protect you forever." Josiah holds his breath. "I can offer you freedom. You would be free to go anywhere you want. Say anything you want and do whatever you want. Freedom is getting what you want, no matter what," Scarlett whispers in his ears. Josiah swallows hard not daring to even move a muscle. The ground shakes again, and more dirt falls in on his head. "Blasted boy. Don't you want freedom?"

He closes his eyes, trying not to get dirt in them. He starts to think about what the word freedom truly means. He knows without hesitation that it doesn't mean what Scarlett says because it has limitations. He shivers; one cannot have true freedom without boundaries and righteousness. "I will leave you to ponder these words. But remember, boy, I will offer you the world. Trust me." The ground shakes, and a blast of dirt falls on Josiah back. Soon, he can hear the birds, and he climbs out of the hole cautiously.

A haze of dust floats in the air above him. He crawls fully out of the hole and starts to climb the hill again.

As Josiah reaches the top of the hill, a huge field filled with giant boulders and stones appear. "This must be the

Stone Maze of Knowledge. I made it." He runs down the path toward the stones.

As he nears the boulders, he can see many people coming and going, but none of them seem to be getting anywhere. They all seem to be dazed and confused. His blood grows cold when he hears a lady scream. People start running in circles, yelling, "Run. She's coming. She'll destroy us if we can't find the right way through." Josiah looks over his shoulder, and he can see What looks like Scarlett in the distance. He runs towards the entrance of the maze. At the entrance, he reads: "Beware. Enter at your own risk. Use wisdom as your guide, choose carefully or die."

Josiah swallows hard as people scatter in several directions. He hides just inside the entrance as he hears, "run." Josiah runs deeper into the maze.

Soon, Josiah comes to a divide in the path. He must make a choice to turn left or right. "Which way should I go?" He paces back and forth a few times; he notices two signs where the divide starts. He reads, "For all have sinned, and come short of the glory of God." He sees another sign. It reads, "We can all reach perfection as time evolves. We share too. We don't need anyone but ourselves." Josiah thinks about it. "This must be a riddle," he tells himself. He looks at the other people, they all are entering the path to perfection, but they all seem to be going in circles.

"I don't need anyone," a man says.

"Perfection is the key," another says. Josiah looks at all of them, and they seem empty and lost. He walks back to the first sign. "For all have sinned and come short of the glory of God." Josiah squares his shoulders and walks down this trail.

There are many twists and turns among this maze. He occasionally sees others along the same path. All seem very sure of themselves and confident with their choice. Then, he comes to two more signs. "For the wages of sin is death, but the gift of God is eternal life through Jesus Christ, our Lord."

Josiah thinks about what this is saying. "The punishment that we earn for our sins and wrong choices is death. Not just physically but eternal death." Josiah shakes nervously at the thought.

He turns to read the second sign, "For the more wages you earn, the happier you will become." Josiah thinks about this sign. It definitely sounds more hopeful, but if Josiah really thinks about his true self, he knows that he's not courageous or powerful on his own. He remembers Scarlett and the kids at her party. They were all about having fun and playing games, and yes, even about winning, but they all looked lost, sad, and pale. The thought sends a shiver down his body.

"I work hard. I earn my wages," a lady says, "but does money make me happy?"

"The more money I make, the more friends I have," a man says back to her.

"Yes, but are they really friends with you, or with your money?" the two toss questions back and forth.

Josiah can hear the beast growl in the distance. He closes his eyes and sits down. Praying, he says, "God, show me the right way. I want to be true to You."

He's startled out of his thoughts and prayers when he hears a lady shout, "I got it. I know the right way." The lady runs down the trail of wages, screams, and then all goes quiet. He swallows hard and watches many more take the same path and disappear, some even returned to the same place even more scared and bruised. The beast is still growling, and people can still be heard screaming in the distance.

Josiah's courage grows as he stands up and rereads the first sign, "For the wages of sin is death, but the gift of God is eternal life through Jesus Christ, our Lord." Josiah nods his head and makes his choice. The path is narrow and hard to maneuver, but he manages to find his way to another set of signs. Before he's able to read them, the hairs on the back of his neck stand up, and he feels cold.

He walks up to the two new signs and reads them loudly. The first sign reads, "Love is fleeting and destructive. Go it alone, and you will be protected. Live for today, tomorrow will worry about itself," *Hmmm,* Josiah wonders about this.

"But God demonstrates His own love for us, in that while we were still sinners, Christ died for us." Josiah looks back and forth between the two signs. "If I go on my own feelings, then yes, love is fleeting and hurtful, but being alone is not good either. That does not bring protection." Josiah thinks some more. "Jesus Christ died for me? He paid my penalty because he loved me. Jesus came back to life, and this proves that God accepted Jesus' death as a price paid for my sins. While I was still His enemy and I hated Him, He still loved me enough to save me." Josiah is overwhelmed with this truth.

In his head, Scarlett says, "I can help you. Come with me, Jo. I can make your life easy. Just follow me."

Josiah shakes his head and pushes the voice off in the distance. "This must be the right way." Josiah chooses the second path and runs down it. He can hear the voice yell, "No!"

Josiah runs around another bend and almost falls over another set of signs. He regains his balance and reads the first sign. "If you show what your greatest strengths are and devote in believing in yourself, you will thrive." *That seems right.* Josiah reads the second sign. "That if you confess with your mouth Jesus as Lord, and believe in your heart that God raised Him from the dead, you will be saved."

"If Jesus died for me, all I have to do is believe? Trust that His death has paid for my sins and I will be saved?"

The first sign leads down a narrow path, but the second sign is just on a boulder and Josiah falls to his knees once again, saying, "I'm a sinner. I do believe in you, Jesus. Only You can save me." The ground shakes, and when he looks up, there is a new path before him. "Thank you," he whispers as he stands and walks through. The ground shakes again, and when Josiah regains his stance, the boulder has closed behind him. "Ok, I guess the only way to go now is forward."

Josiah's steps get harder and harder as the hill gets steeper. Leaning on some of the boulders and small trees growing around him, pulls himself along the edge. He reaches into his pocket and pulls out a carabineer that he got from camp, unlaces one of his shoes, and makes a small anchor to brace himself as he rests a little. The hill gets so steep he is nearly forced to crawl to continue. He sees another two signs come into view. So, he unhooks his carabineer and bunches up his shoelace, stuffing both into his pocket again as he crawls to the next signs. "God loves you so much, and He is holy. Therefore, if you make a mistake, your sin will be revealed. You will lose your connection with God and be separated from him forever." The other sign reads, "Therefore, there is no condemnation for those who are in Christ Jesus, for I am convinced that neither death nor life, neither angels nor demons, neither the present nor the future, nor any powers, neither height nor depth, nor anything else in all creation, will be able to separate us from the love of God that is in Christ Jesus our Lord." Josiah thinks about this. *There is a lot to think about in both of these signs.* He thinks, *I'm not perfect, and I do mess up a lot, but will a Holy God who cannot be around sin still accept me? Or will I be forever separated from Him?* He shivers at the thought.

"I don't ever want to take the easy road if it means separating myself from God." Josiah compares both paths. The one the first sign leads to slants downward and evens out and might be an easier climb, but the second trail is still leading upward with big stones and loose gravel. "Well, I was never told this would be easy." He shrugs and continues his upward climb. He's tired and gasping for breath.

After a few more hours of this painful, steep, rocky climb, he can see a sign up ahead with a rope hanging down from it and another sign that is just sitting on the ground, as if someone had knocked it down and stomped on it. He feels defeated, tired, and out of energy. He does not even want to read the second sign. What if it is worse? I am not sure if I could handle the rejection. What other people tell me or say about me, reflects who I am. Right? He falls to his knees once again. "God, I feel so defeated, broken. I have nothing to offer. I just don't know what to do."

His hand falls to the ground and when he blinks his eyes to clear his vision, he notices that his hand is on the sign that is fallen on the ground. "For I know the plans I have for you, declares the Lord. Plans to prosper you and not to harm you, plans to give you hope and a future."

When he looks toward the first sign, it reads, "Treasure and gold I give to you, money and power you will rule it all. Worship me, and you will not be defeated." Josiah scratches his head and thinks about everything he has been saved from and how far in his journey he has come.

"No, I worship the God of heaven and earth. He is the one true God and I will serve no other." Josiah says with authority he never knew he had. "God, I need you, I believe in You and You alone." Josiah prays. He turns and walks the rest of the way towards the second sign.

He finds himself exiting the maze of knowledge on the other side. "Thank God. Thank You for helping me and for always being with me. I will never give up." Josiah jumps for joy because he found the knowledge he needed to make the hard choices.

He looks ahead. There is a huge, thick forest, and he reads a sign, "The Forest of Truth." He gasps. Josiah looks at the forest before him. To his left, there are many fallen branches, a trickling stream, and lots of debris. He turned to his right and sees fallen trees and rotting pieces of wood. "There seems to be no end or way around this forest."

Josiah pushes his way through the trees and stumbles past them. It's dark and hard to maneuver. He remembers his flashlight dangling from his belt loop. He pulls it loose and shines it around. *At least dad thought of something useful,* he thinks.

As Josiah's eyes adjust to the light, he sees the fallen trees and uneven mossy ground. The air about him is damp and cold. As he steps, the moss squishes under his feet. Suddenly, he jumps at the sight of a shadow moving to his right, and he shines his light in the direction of the shadow, but it's gone.

"When I am weak, God is my strength. I will not give up. I choose to follow truth." Josiah reminds himself. He feels courage growing within him. He brushes off his clothes and takes a deep breath, "I have the wisdom of Christ, and He is my guide," he says.

He jumps at the muffled sound of a voice not too far away. He turns off his flashlight and slowly moves towards the sounds to investigate, trying to be as quiet as possible.

"I just have so many questions." As Josiah piers from the branches he can see the silhouette of a blonde haired woman who seems to be talking on the phone. "Tell me again, where are Kat and Crystal?" She pauses to listen. Josiah tiptoes closer to get a better look, the woman's back is turned towards him. "Ok, how was Delores involved?"

The woman starts to pace nervously as she listens on. "But how could my niece betray me like that? Wait, what? What do you mean a new threat? You are changing the subject. What do you mean things will become clearer? Lucas, I need clarity and answers. There just seems like a lot of dead ends lately. No, you stop. You need to hear me out. Forget about this Nora person, I thought I was the important one. I am ordering you back. No, I mean now." The woman stops and stomps her foot. "Meet me at the castle. I want to discuss this further. Yes, now. I require a face to face meeting." The woman hangs up her phone and looks around.

"Ok, I have started the ball rolling. Forest of truth, please, the fog is lifting some, but I fear when I leave this forest it will come back. Help me not to forget again. I need to confront Lucas." Josiah watches on as the woman heads towards the edge of the forest from which he had just entered. Just before she steps out she turns slightly and he gets a glimpse of Scarlett's face as she vanishes from sight.

"What? What is going on here?" Josiah says as he turns to go deeper into the forest, he catches his foot on a tree stump and rolls down a hill.

He shines his flashlight around to inspect his surroundings. He's standing at the bottom of a hill, surrounded by thick trees. "Well, I can't go up the hill, so I guess I keep heading forward."

He carefully takes a few more steps. His flashlight is the only thing that provides enough light for Josiah to see where to place his next step. He shivers as he feels the temperature drop and he notices that he's no longer walking over fallen leaves but crunching upon snow. He shines his flashlight ahead where he sees movement. He cautiously peers through, and his mind starts to race. Questions start running in and out of his mind. What is this movement? Is it friendly? Do I dare make my presence known? What if it's Scarlett? He shakes his head and decides to move forward.

To Josiah's surprise, it's not Scarlett at all. "Hey there, Jo. Long time no see."

"What? Wait? Trevor? But."

"Take it easy, little bro. You're not dead."

"But...."

"Yes, I am. I needed to talk to you. You need to understand the truth."

"Truth? What do you mean? Truth?"

"Ok, first of all, breathe. You're safe."

Josiah takes a few deep breaths, turns off his flashlight, and leans against a large tree stump. "Trevor, I don't understand. If you're dead, and I'm not, how is this possible?"

"I know this is confusing for you, but this is the forest of truth, where the truth will set you free. You just need to understand the truth, and I am the best person to clarify it for you. Do you trust me?"

"You know I have always trusted you. But what truth do I need to understand? Will this help me find Nora? You know how angry she is with what happened between you and Bobbie."

"Please don't blame Bobbie. He has been through enough. You need to show both Bobbie and Nora forgiveness and understanding."

"I try to understand Bobbie, but he's so bitter and rude."

"Bobbie's what he knows. Do you know what happened that night?"

"Just that you went to Bobbie's, and the next thing I hear is there were shots fired and you were dead." Josiah slides down the side of the stump and sits in the snow. The tears slide freely down his face. "Please, Trevor, help me understand. Did Bobbie shoot you? Was there a robbery and you got caught in the crossfire?"

"You're partly right. But there was no robbery. I saved Bobbie's life."

"What? How? And why would you do that?" Josiah feels the sadness and anger boiling in his blood. He clenches his fists. "Why? Why did you have to die?"

Josiah feels Trevor's hand rest on his shoulder. "Do you remember Bobbie's dad?"

"That crazy old coot? Of course, I remember, but he's in jail now."

"That was after I died."

"The night I went to see Bobbie. We were downstairs, and I heard fighting upstairs. Bobbie ran upstairs to see what was going on."

"I heard all this before; someone broke into the house and went after Bobbie's mom."

"Jo, that someone was Bobbie's dad. He started beating Bobbie and threw him down the stairs."

"Wait…What? That was not in the police report."

"It wouldn't be. Bobbie's mom asked for that part not be mentioned."

"But what happened?"

"It was instinct, I guess. I ran to Bobbie's side to see is if he was ok. As I knelt down beside him, I saw a foot fly at my face. Next thing I knew, the shots of pain as several blows of a foot plunged into my stomach, blood dripping from my mouth and eyes."

"Trevor, what do you mean?"

"Bobbie grabbed his dad's gun. Bobbie's dad lifted me up as a human shield and threw me at Bobbie. The gun went off, and as I started to black out, Bobbie's dad laughed and told Bobbie that he brought this on himself. I could hear Bobbie yell at his dad as he started to dial the emergency number. 'Look, boy. If you mention I was here, then your mother's death will be on you as well,' I heard Bobbie's dad say. The door slammed shut from up stairs as sirens became louder. 'Hang in there.' was the last I heard from Bobbie. "

Josiah's face turns red with anger. "Why tell me this? How does it help? It doesn't bring you back."

"No, but Bobbie blames himself. My death saved his life."

"Yes, but at what cost?"

"You need to learn the truth of his pain. He's scared to let anyone close. You need to fight for his soul. Don't you see this pain will not only destroy him but you and Nora as well? If you cannot learn to forgive, how will healing rise up?"

"I miss your wisdom, Trevor."

"This truth needs to be understood. Yes, there's pain with truth, but you are stronger than you think. Never give up on yourself, on God's love for you, on Nora, but most importantly on the truth." Trevor holds out his hand to help Josiah to his feet. "Your journey isn't over, but you need to keep moving forward, one step at a time. Nora needs you, and you need her. Don't allow yourself to be pushed away. Nora is hurting too, and she keeps pushing her feelings down within herself and hides herself away."

"Trevor, what do you want from me?"

Trevor pulls Josiah close into a hug and whispers, "Believe in the truth, and the truth will set you free." Suddenly, Josiah is standing alone. He turns and takes ten more steps and finds his way out of the forest.

A blast of wind propels him forward and he struggles to stay on his feet. "Nnnnoooooo!" He turns to see a flash of silver retreating into the forest, he dizzily pants for breath. As he looks around, he sees a big open field surrounded by a wall of trees. "Keep going, Josiah." He encourages himself as he walks through the field.

Trevor's voice returns: "You are stronger than you think. Never lose heart."

He takes a deep breath and smiles. "Thanks for revealing the truth to me." He turns and starts to cross the field. From his journey so far, what may seem easy is not always true.

The sun is shining, and the air smells sweet. The grain is growing and swaying in the wind. He could hear an eagle calling, almost as reassurance or reminder that he's not alone.

PART 3

The Risk Is Real

CHAPTER 7

The Peaceful River

As Senora sits, resting her eyes under the bridge, she listens to the Peaceful River. Suddenly, she hears something new break through the sounds: laughter and footsteps. Someone's coming. She hides further under the bridge and listens to who it may be. She's scared because she doesn't know if those men chasing her had discovered that she ran to the Peaceful River.

Josiah's excited that he has at last found the Peaceful River. He walks onto the bridge.

With a deep breath and sigh, he says, "I will find you, Nora." His voice is light enough to be a whisper.

"Jo?" someone says his name. "Is that you?" He looks around and notices movement from under the bridge.

"Who's there?" Josiah calls out. He sees Senora climb out from under the bridge. "Nora!" He runs to the end of the bridge as Senora runs up the hill to meet him. They both hug each other. "I thought I would never find you. You wouldn't believe what I've been through." Josiah breathes a sigh of relief.

Senora opens her mouth to say something when she hears the quads in the distance. "There's no time," she says as she grabs Josiah's hand and runs down the hill to hide under the bridge. Josiah and Senora hear rumbling as the quads slow to a stop in the middle of the bridge. They both kneel as they hear footsteps above them.

"Keep a look out, men. She has to be around here somewhere. I'm sure she couldn't have gone any farther." Senora shivers at the sound of Lucas' voice. They can hear people walk back and forth from one end of the bridge to the other. Josiah sees some small rocks fall off the bridge into the water. Senora holds her breath in fear.

"The boss is too powerful, sir. This girl, Nora, is it? Yes, Nora, she's nothing. The boss always gets what she wants," another says.

"Don't even mention the boss. She scares me," Lucas says. "I know we're close." Senora sees another clump of rocks fall into the water.

Senora shivers when she hears the roar of the red dragon again. "Oh, no," Lucas says, "We need to go. Now."

"Why? Are we supposed to..." The second man's voice fades away. Josiah and Senora see the red dragon fly over the bridge as the quads speed away.

"Ummmm, what just happened?" Josiah asks as he turns to face Senora.

"Well, at least it scared away those men. They have been chasing me," Senora says.

"What do they want?" Josiah asks.

"I honestly don't know. They captured me once and were questioning me about the Hills of Courage and about a treasure. When I escaped, one man called Lucas, the leader who was talking up there a few minutes ago, told me that I would never find this treasure, and I would never win. But I didn't know what he was talking about." Senora lets out a huge sigh. "The lady I met at the beginning of this journey, Sam, spoke of a treasure that I must find. Jo, I have been so mean and selfish towards you. I'm sorry."

"Nora, we have both said things. Can you forgive me?"

"Of course, Jo. I love you. I'll always forgive you."

"I forgive and love you too, Nora." They hug again.

Josiah remembers something Senora said to him earlier. "I also heard whispers of a treasure, the Greatest Treasure," Josiah says to Senora.

"Sam found me in a place called the forgetful woods. I saw a girl; she was skating and singing as if in a dream," Senora says.

"I was also told that we would both need to combine what we learned up to now," Josiah says, in a hushed voice.

"What have we learned?" Senora feels heavy at the thought of her journey. She remembers Sam speaking about a treasure. "The kingdom of heaven is like treasure hidden in a field, which a man found and covered up. Then in his joy he goes and sells all that he has and buys that field.[52] ... Find the Greatest Treasure."

Josiah ponders Senora words, and he thinks about his journey so far. "You won't be the same after your journey. Never give up. He gives power to the faint, and to him who has no might, He increases; but they who wait for the Lord shall renew their strength; they shall mount up with wings like eagles; they shall run and not be faint.[53]"

"So, the one who leads us is the Lord?" Senora asks. "Even when we hide, He sees us and is with us?"

"Yes, also when we're scared or tired. He'll give us strength."

---

[52] Matthew 13:44
[53] Isaiah 40:29, 31

"'I will never leave you nor forsake you.'[54] You'll need each other, you both, together must discover the Greatest Treasure," Senora says.

"So, we need to keep focused. Our journey is not over. He's always with us; we must not allow money or things to distract us," says Josiah, "I wonder what the Greatest Treasure is, and what is the key for? Are you up for a new adventure?"

"Those men could still be out there, but I know that we are stronger together," Senora says.

"Ok, what else have you learned so far, Nora?"

"Friendship is a bond, but family is unbreakable," Senora remembers Sam's words. "For you formed my inward parts; you knit me together in my mother's womb. I praise you, for I am fearfully and wonderfully made. Wonderful are your works; my soul knows it very well. My frame was not hidden from you, when I was being made in secret intricately woven in the depths of the earth.[55]" Senora feels a tear trickle down her cheek as she remembers Trevor.

"For the wages of sin is death, but the gift of God is eternal life through Jesus Christ our Lord. But God demonstrates His love for us, in that while we were still sinners, Christ died for us. That if we confess with our mouth Jesus as Lord, and believe in our hearts that God raised Him from the dead, we will be saved. Therefore, there is no condemnation for those who are in Christ Jesus. He loves you Nora, and He forgives you. Do you believe?" Josiah asks.

"I do believe. I believe He loves me and even when I hated Him, He still loved me." Senora looks at Josiah with tears in her eyes. How she will perceive her past is her choice. "I can tell you one thing: my past mistakes and perspectives are all lies. God doesn't make garbage and, He never makes mistakes.

---

[54] Hebrews 13:5b
[55] Psalm 139:13-15

Everything that God makes is beautiful. Yes, even mosquitoes, even though I don't like them."

"I love you, Nora. You're my little sister. God calls us to turn away from our bad behaviour. We need to be strong in His strength now. Never give up." Josiah hugs his sister as she cries a little into his shoulder.

"Nora? Can you forgive Bobbie and what happened with Trevor too?"

Senora feels a lump in her throat. She knows and understands now that if she holds onto her anger, she will lose who she really is. "It'll be hard, but yes. I'll need God's help for me to forgive what happened. I miss Trevor so much."

"I understand. I miss him too."

"Thank you, Jo." Suddenly, they're both startled by the sound of growling. "What's that?" Josiah asks.

"We need to be brave," Senora says to Josiah.

"But what is it? It must be big and scary. Those men took off quite fast when they heard it," he reminds her.

"Yes, but something tells me to look into it. The growl doesn't sound that far away." Senora holds out her hand towards Josiah and stands up with confidence in her eyes. "Together?"

Josiah takes his sisters hand, swallows hard, and nods. "I'm with you. Never give up." They both make their way out from under the bridge and climb the hill, listening intently for any danger. "There it is again." They run across the bridge and down the road. The growling gets louder with each step. Josiah stops when he hears thumping and banging.

"It's down there toward the Peaceful River," he whispers to his sister. She nods, and they tiptoe to the side of the road where they can overlook the river. Their eyes get huge at the sight. Never before had either of them seen anything like it.

The body was as big as a bus and was red from the tip of its nose down to the end of its tail, long, and covered in scales. Four legs as big as oak tree stumps as it thrashed about with sharp claws and a long tail that swayed back and forth like a giant snake moving in the grass. The head was the width of a car, with six pointed horns upon it. A piercing growl so loud that they had to cover their ears.

Josiah wants to run, but he's frozen with fear. He feels Senora put her hand on his shoulder. "Be brave. He gives strength to the faint and weary."

Senora stands up and starts to walk towards the beast. "The Lord is my light and my salvation; whom shall I fear?[56]" Senora says.

The beast growls again and swings its mighty tail toward Senora. She ducks and the tail misses her. The beast swings its tail back, and she jumps over it. "Easy there. I won't hurt you." Senora sees the beast calm down and she looks into its big, emerald green eyes. They look sad and angry at the same time. It has a long snout like a crocodile. Senora squares her shoulders and takes a deep breath. "Who are you?" she asks bravely.

The beast growls again, and Senora covers her ears. It swings its tail again, and Senora jumps over. The beast looks at Senora and then looks down to lick at its foot. Senora notices that there's something stuck in the beast's foot. She puts her hand in front of her and walks toward the beast. "Careful. Easy. I can help you." The beast looks up at Senora. Senora makes her way until she is now standing right next to it. It's as tall as a two-story building. Senora shivers, but she knows she can help. "Jo, I need your help," she says over her shoulder. The beast looks up to where Josiah is now standing. "Slowly come towards me. Be brave."

Josiah cautiously walks toward the beast. "Are you sure it's safe?"

"No, but I cannot do this on my own. I need your help. It's hurt, and we must help it."

---

[56] Psalm 27:1a

Josiah carefully approaches his sister and the beast. "God is with us, and we will trust Him no matter what happens. Right?"

Senora takes Josiah's hands, and they both reach out together to pull what looks like an arrow. The beast growls in pain and swings its tail violently. As the two pull, they can feel the arrow come loose. The two of them fall backwards with the arrow in their hands, and the beast growls so loud that their ears ring. It spreads out its giant red wings and disappears into the clouds. They are left lying on their backs, holding the arrow in their hands and staring up at the sky. They hear an eagle call and the water of the river. Josiah takes the arrow from Senora and stands up. He throws it into the tall grass and holds out his hand to help Senora up.

"What was that Nora? Do you think it's gone for good?"

"The Red Dragon. But I have a feeling we just made a friend." The two look up at the sky once more and smile. They crawl back up the hill and continue to walk down the road.

"How did you know the beast wouldn't hurt you?"

Senora shrugs. "I guess because I was trusting God's peaceful leading."

"I have seen some sort of beast along my travels too, but I don't think it is the same one," Josiah says.

"What are you saying, Jo? Do you mean there's more than one dragon?" Senora fills with excitement.

"I think so. During the first encounter, I caught a glimpse of the dragon. It was not red. It was silver. Does that make sense?"

"I think so." Senora looks around.

"But I don't carry the same excitement as you do." Josiah sighs.

"Why not, Jo?" Senora asks.

"Well, the Red Dragon sounds like it has been helping and guiding you, right?"

"Yes, that's right, Jo. What are you getting at?"

"Well, the Silver Dragon more seemed to torment me." Jo looks concerned at his sister.

"It's ok, Jo. We have God protecting us." She tries to smile to reassure him. "Come on, Jo. We have a treasure to find." Senora holds out her hand to encourage Josiah to walk with her. He takes a deep breath, feeling peace and comfort come over him.

CHAPTER 8

Determine Your Destination

As they walk over the next rise in the road, Josiah sees the tall bearded man. He looks up, smiles, waves, and both Josiah and Senora walk up to him.

"Who's this?" The man points at Senora.

"This is my sister, Nora," Josiah says.

"Are you ready to discover what the Greatest Treasure is?" the man asks.

"Yes! But where do we go from here?" Josiah asks as Senora looks at the man suspiciously.

"Do not lay up for yourselves treasures on earth, where moth and rust destroy and where thieves break in and steal, but lay up for yourselves treasures in heaven, where neither moth nor rust destroys and where thieves do not break in and steal. For where your treasure is, there your heart will be also.[57]" Josiah scratches his head and ponders the man's words. "The good person out of the good treasure of his heart produces good.[58]."

Senora listens intently to the man's words and considers what the Greatest Treasure really is. "But we have this treasure in jars of clay, to show that the surpassing power belongs to God and not to us.[59]" The man continues and says, "They are to do good, to be rich in good works, to be generous and ready to share, thus storing up treasure for themselves as a good foundation for the future, so that they may take hold of that which is truly life.[60] For we are His workmanship, created in Christ Jesus for good works, which God prepared beforehand, that we should walk in them.[61]" He stops and smiles. "Consider these words; they will help you along your journey. I'm glad you found your sister. You will need each other. Remember never give up hope."

"Thank you, but we do not know where to go from here," Josiah says. The man looks puzzled.

"For the gate is narrow and the way is hard that leads to life, and those who find it are few.[62]."

"Nora, if we work together, we can discover what this treasure is."

"But how? We don't know where to go," Senora says with slumped shoulders.

Then, she remembers Sam's words: "Follow the way of the Red Dragon."

"We are not alone, and we did not know our way to each other and yet, we found one another. We can do this. Are you

---

[57]   Matthew 6:19-20
[58]   Luke 6:45a
[59]   2 Corinthians 4:7
[60]   1 Timothy 6:18-19
[61]   Ephesians 2:10
[62]   Matthew 7:14

game?" Josiah holds out his hand. She squares her shoulders, nods her head, and places her hand on top of Josiah's.

"Let's do this," she says with confidence. "Friendship is a bond, but family is unbreakable."

Their ears ring again as they hear the roar of the Red Dragon. "Jo, we need to follow the way of the Red Dragon." As they turn and see the Red Dragon weaving in and out of the clouds, they both jump at the clap of thunder as the storm clouds roll in.

The bearded man waves and is gone. "Good luck and may the Lord be with you," his voice whispers in their ears.

"Ummm, where did he go?" Senora asks. As she looks, she sees a small backpack sitting where the man had previously been standing.

"I don't know, but he tends to do that a lot." He looks at Senora and bends down to pick up the back pack and reads, "These should help you along the way." He shrugs and pulls the backpack over one shoulder.

"You ready?" he asks.

"Yes." Senora pats her brother on the back gently.

Senora looks in the direction they saw the flash of red and jumps a little at the sight of the thick black clouds upon hearing a clap of thunder. Senora looks up at the clouds nervously as the sky gets darker and darker. "Do you think it might rain?"

"It might, but God will protect us," Josiah reassures her. Senora fills with courage and smiles at Josiah. They walk up a hill away from the Peaceful River. Josiah looks up with a start when he sees a flash of lightning. "Ok, let's go." He looks over his shoulder at Senora. He gives her a smile and thumbs up to encourage her. Senora smiles and gives a nod and thumbs up back at him. Not long afterwards, the rain starts to come down. The mud is slushy and slippery. Josiah raises his hand above his eyes so he can see better. In the distance he sees a small shelter made of wood. He points, and says, "There." He grabs Senora's hand and they crawl into the shelter.

"It looks like an old tree fort," Senora says.

"At least it's dry. We can wait here until the rain stops," Josiah says. He pulls the backpack off his back, opens it up, and pulls out one of the water bottles. He tosses it to Senora. "Here, you must be thirsty." He pulls out another and takes a small drink.

Senora catches the water bottle and takes a drink too. "Thanks, Jo." She pants as she catches her breath. Senora remembers the backpack Sam had given her. Those men must have confiscated it when they had captured her. She was thankful for the short time that she did have it and fills with gratitude in knowing that they have this backpack to use. They both close their eyes to rest.

Josiah is startled awake by the sound of an eagle call. He squints as the sun beams shines through the cracks in the wood. He coughs as he takes a deep breath of dusty, musty air. With the sun shining in, he sees his surroundings much better. The fort Senora and he took refuge in the night before has just enough room for the two of them to sit toe to toe as they each rest their backs on the outer wooden walls. It's a small fort with a mud floor, and the walls are made of old wooden pallets. He gently leans over and taps Senora on the shoulder. "Nora, it's time to wake up," Josiah whispers. She awakes with a start at hearing her brother's voice. She yawns and rubs her eyes. "We should keep going. The rain has stopped."

They crawl out of the opening of the tree fort, stand up, and look around. The sun feels warm upon their faces and they notice they are surrounded by bright green, leafy trees.

Senora looks around. The night before when they walked through the rain, she could only see Josiah. She couldn't see where they were until now. Now, with the sun shining brightly, she's almost frozen with fear. Panic fills her heart "JJJo…" The words get stuck in her throat. She swallows hard and tries again. "JJJo…wwwait!"

Josiah stops in his tracks and turns. "What is it, Nora?" He notices that his sister's face has gone white.

"I just realized where we are." Her voice is barely above a whisper.

"What? Where? Nora, you look like you have just seen a hurricane coming your way."

"We're near that building where those men took me. Oh, Jo. I cannot get caught again, especially when I still do not know what they want."

Josiah walks over to Senora and puts his hand on her shoulder. "Be brave. Just think they don't know we're here. This gives us an advantage." Josiah motions to Senora to follow him around a nearby small rock building. "Shshshsh, I think I hear something," Josiah whispers. They crouch down, sneak around the rock building, and stop when they hear people talking.

"I know that we'll find her. Yes Ma'am. I won't give up. You'll always be the queen. Yes, but. Don't worry. They won't discover the truth. The princess will not be found. She is skating. Yes still. She is still in your power. She won't wake up. Yes, I know but. Yes, Ma'am. I'll find her. Good bye." Lucas hangs up his phone and turns to talk to two other men who are standing with him.

"What's the order? What did the boss say?" one man asks.

"We need to find Nora. Before it's too late!"

"But that beast. Is it protecting her or hunting her?"

"We can't worry about the beast right now. The queen is concerned about this Nora girl. She holds a power within her. The queen fears her and says if she makes it to the treasure then all she has built will be lost."

"We can't let that happen," the third man says.

"I know."

"But the beast," the second says.

"I know that too."

"I did hit it with an arrow, but I'm not sure if that stopped it," Lucas says.

Senora leans back against the wall and swallows hard. Josiah turns and motions for Senora to follow him. They walk back to the tree fort. "Oh, Jo. What do we do?" Senora asks. He can see her hug her knees.

"I don't know." He looks at her and sighs. "Nora? What did they mean about you having a power within?"

"I honestly don't know. Why did they ask if the beast might be protecting me?"

"Maybe if I approach them saying that I know you they can take me, and I can find out more information about this queen they were talking about," Josiah says.

"But she sounds mean and dangerous. What if they hurt you? I couldn't let that happen."

"Yes, but if they think that I'm useful and helping them, then they won't hurt me. Those guards seem to know a lot. I could maybe join them to find out what they actually know and reconnect with you later."

"But if you're with them then what do I do?" Josiah scratches his head. The idea of going in with the possibility of being discovered and not having Senora close for backup didn't appeal to him. He also knew that they needed to find this treasure. Senora reminds him. "If we split up again we are more likely to get captured, and we're more vulnerable alone."

"You're right, but what do you suggest?" Senora thinks about it, and she remembers her friend Samantha.

"Wait. When I was caught last time there was a lady who helped me escape. Her name is Sam. She seemed to know her way around the building. There's just one problem."

"What?"

"I don't know how to find her. She's always been the one to find me."

Josiah considers how to find Samantha and what they should do. "You say she always finds you. Right?"

"Yeah, what are you hinting at?"

"Well, if we do separate, do you think Samantha might help me?"

"I don't know." Senora looks worried. "I don't want to chance anything happening to you or you getting hurt, or worse killed. I don't know what to do, but Jo, I do know we need to stay together," Senora whispers. Josiah holds up his hand and listens. They hear footsteps.

"Someone's coming," Josiah whispers. They hear quads driving around again, and the footsteps quicken. They hear the quads fade off and see the silhouette of someone standing right beside the fort, panting heavily.

Senora piers through a crack in the fort wall, but she can't make out the person crouching outside. Josiah taps Senora on the shoulder. He motions that he is going to peek out. Senora shakes her head no, but she knows they do need to do something. So, eventually, she agrees.

As Josiah moves to crawl out of the fort opening, Senora sees the figure outside turn to face the entrance. Senora moves to stop Josiah but it's too late.

Josiah crawls out, and as he turns his head to see who's outside, he sees a big stick coming towards his face, and then, all goes black.

CHAPTER 9

Pass Through the Waters

Senora shakes with fear as her brother lies knocked out before her. She starts to cry, fearing the worst. Suddenly, she sees Samantha look inside. "Nora? What are you doing here? I thought you went to the Peaceful River? " Senora is startled to see Samantha.

"Oh, Sam. I did go to the Peaceful River. Why did you knock out Jo, my brother?" Senora asks.

"Oops. I'm sorry, Nora. Here, help me move him. When I heard movement, I just reacted. I'm sorry I didn't see who it was until after I hit him. But he cannot be seen." Senora wipes her tears away with her sleeve and climbs over her brother. As the two girls grab an arm each and drag him around the rock building, Senora notices blood dripping down Samantha's arm.

"Sam, what happened to your arm?" Senora asks.

"Not important, not important," Samantha says. "You need to stay focused on the task at hand. Don't worry about me. I'll be fine." Samantha pulls the backpack off Josiah's back; she opens it and pulls out one of the water bottles and a blanket. She pours the water over the corner of the blanket and dabs it over Josiah's forehead.

Josiah feels the wetness and slowly opens his eyes. He sees Senora and a red-haired lady looking over him. He sits up, and his head starts to spin. He rubs his throbbing forehead. "Ow. Are you crazy? That really hurt."

"Are you ok, Jo?" Senora sounds worried. He decides to reassure her with a nod of the head and a smile.

"My head hurts, and I feel a little dizzy, but I'll be fine. Who's this? She sure has a strong swing, *that* I am sure of," Josiah says hoarsely as he rests his head against the wall and closes his eyes.

"This is my friend, Sam."

"You know, you are pretty tough." She punches Josiah playfully in the shoulder. Josiah coughs a little and smiles. "But you cannot be here," Samantha says.

Senora swallows hard and takes a deep breath. "We're following the way of the Red Dragon, like you said."

"I saw the dragon's path heading to the Forgetful Woods, you know, Nora, where I originally found you. Until I found you there, I didn't think anyone knew where it was, except me."

"You must go. Beware of the Queen. Anyone who crosses her path is destined for no good. But even worse if you run into Lucas. He says he serves her, but I'm not sure. He's full of deceit and lies. If you meet him, he'll try to trick you and distract you from your journey. Stay strong. You need each other for support. Don't let yourselves become divided. You'll need one another to find the treasure. The queen must have known this." Samantha rises to her feet and looks around.

"Remember always that friendship is a bond, but family is unbreakable."

"Yes, Sam, I remember. Will you come with us?"

Samantha shakes her head. "No, that's not my journey, but I will be there when you need me. You and Jo need to do this." She looks at Josiah. "I'm sorry about your head." Josiah rubs his head again and winces.

"It's alright. I'll be fine," He says to reassure both girls.

"Trust in the Lord with all your heart, and do not lean on your own understanding. In all your ways acknowledge Him, and He will make straight your paths.[63] Head towards that tree line and look for the Red Dragon flying low over a narrow path. Wait until dark and the guards will not see you at that time. They are still looking for you, Nora, by the Peaceful River. That gives you an advantage. Once you get into the trees, you'll be safer." Samantha shakes Josiah's hand and nods at Senora. She smiles, turns, and runs over the hill toward the Peaceful River and disappears out of sight.

"How will we know the right way to go?" Josiah asks.

"The Red Dragon will show us the way when we need direction, Jo. It makes sense to get into the cover of the trees so that we're not seen as easily. Right?"

"I guess you're right, Nora."

"And besides, what choice do we have anyway?"

"True."

As the sun starts to set, they hear the quads return. Senora peeks around the building. She sees the men dismount their quads and go into the main building. She turns to look at her brother. "How's your head?" she asks.

"Better. Did they catch Sam?"

"I didn't see her. Can you run? The guards are all inside. Now is our chance." Josiah nods and Senora helps him to his feet. "Ok, on three, we run toward the trees. *Three.*" The two take off running as the Red Dragon passes over their heads, flying low. Josiah sees the path as they approach the tree line. He grabs Senora's arm, and they fall into the trees and out of sight from the main building.

---

[63] Proverbs 3:5-6

Senora looks through the trees to make sure they were not seen. All looks quiet. She turns and helps Josiah stand up again. He still feels a little dizzy, but he finds his courage and strength. He leans a little on his sister for support as they speed walk down the path.

In the distance, they hear gun fire. Senora's pulse quickens, and she moves faster. "Do you think they saw us?" Josiah asks, panting for breath.

"I don't know. But we must continue. Never give up, Jo." They hear twigs breaking behind them and more gun fire. Josiah fills with adrenaline, and he finds himself running alongside Senora. He runs ahead of her into a clearing as Senora hears quads up ahead. "Jo, wait," Senora calls out. She reaches out her hand to stop him when the quads appear, and Lucas appears from behind Senora. He grabs her while the two quads stop in front of Josiah, shining their lights in his eyes. He falls backward.

"You. Stand up," Lucas calls out to Josiah. "Who are you?" Josiah slowly stands; he looks from his sister to Lucas and back again. "Answer me," Lucas demands. Josiah swallows hard and clears his throat. His head is throbbing, and he feels dizzy again. He opens his mouth to speak when he hears a loud roar. Lucas looks up at the sky in fear. He pushes Josiah to the ground. Senora runs to his side and hugs him. "We cannot lose them now. Stand your ground, men."

"Stay strong, Jo," Senora says. "The Lord is my strength, whom shall I fear." He hears the growl again. "Though I walk through the shadow of death, I will fear no evil. Your rod and Your staff, they comfort me," Josiah hears Senora say. He sees what looks like the Red Dragon land between Senora and the two quads. Then all goes black again. He can hear some screaming and some gun fire. He feels Senora holding him close. A shower of dust flies over him, and the quads drive circles around them. The air he breathes in is so hot, it almost burns his nostrils. He coughs, but he's having trouble opening his eyes. "Hold on, Jo. Be strong. You must find the courage and trust." He hears the Red Dragon growl again, and he feels Senora shaking him. "Jo, Jo. Open your eyes. Find your strength." Senora's almost screaming at him.

Josiah comes to only briefly, and he sees the Red Dragon jumping back and forth, growling loudly. He sees Senora standing with what looks like fire in her eyes. "With man, this is impossible, but with God, all things are possible.[64]" He faints again. Josiah can feel heat upon his face and sweat trickle down his forehead.

He manages to open one eye to see the Red Dragon blowing fire all around them. He hears more gunshots and Lucas barking out orders for everyone to stand firm. Senora talks in a confident and strong voice, one that he has never heard from his sister before. "He gives strength to the weak and power to the powerless," she says. Josiah can see Lucas try to approach him when he sees what looks like the Red Dragon's tail swings and knock Lucas off balance.

Senora raises her hand as the Red Dragon charges at the men on the quads. Josiah feels dizzy as his vision blurs again. The smoke from the surrounding fire makes his throat burn and his eyes sting.

He can hear the Red Dragon growling, and he can also hear the spinning of the quad tires. Someone is moving him, but he is not sure who is doing it. When he opens his eyes again, he sees that he's riding on the back of a quad. He drifts off into sleep once again as the growling fades.

When Josiah wakes again, the sun shines down on him, and he is lying in the grass. Senora is sitting with her back towards him. He reaches out his hand to touch her back. Senora jumps, turns to face Josiah, and hugs him. "I was so worried. I can't lose you like I lost Trevor. You really scared

---

[64] Matthew 19:26

116

me. Are you alright? Please say you're alright." She breathes a sigh of relief.

"Nora? What just happened?" Josiah asks weakly. Senora pulls away and looks Josiah straight in the eye.

"I'm not sure. I remember the Red Dragon and the men fighting. I remember the fear of losing you, and standing, feeling strength grow within me like I have never felt before. I remember pulling you onto the back of the quad and driving away. How are you feeling?"

"Confused, but better. Nora, I'm still here. I'm too stubborn for you to lose me that easily. Is the Red Dragon ok?"

"I think so. I remember it flying away when I drove off on the quad," Senora says.

"Where are we? Have you been awake all night?"

"I drove the quad for a few hours and stopped here to rest. I'm not sure where we are, but I think we're safe. We have been here all night, and all has been quiet," Senora tells him. Josiah sits up to look around. He can see leafy trees far in the distance and to his right a large mountain that seems to stand alone. They're sitting in tall grass and the wind is blowing. He shivers. Senora wraps one of the blankets around him.

"Do you see the path still?" he asks. Senora looks around. She sees the mountain and also notices evergreens to her left. They're in an open field. The grass is worn in some places, but she doesn't see a path.

She frowns and looks at Josiah. "I'm sorry, but I don't."

Josiah looks at his sister. "I remember you standing and saying God's words. You do have power within. I've seen it. God gives strength to the weak and power to the powerless." He takes both of Senora's hands in his. "Let's pray," he says. They look up at the sky. "Dear heavenly Father, we need You. You have been our strength and our guide up to now. Your holiness stretches beyond our imagination. Help us now; we need to find the way."

"Lord Jesus, I love You, and thank You so much for loving me even when I didn't deserve it. We don't know where to go. Please show us the way. Amen."

Josiah hears an eagle call and he sees the Red Dragon flying in the distance. The clouds part and sunbeams shine down. He taps Senora on the shoulder and points toward the dragon. "Follow the path of the Red Dragon, right?" They both stand up. Senora pulls the backpack onto her shoulders, and Josiah folds up his blanket. He puts it back into the backpack and zips it up.

They both look at the quad. "We should leave it. That way they cannot track us as easily," Josiah suggests. Senora agrees, and they turn to walk in the direction they saw the Red Dragon.

As they walk, they see something appear over the horizon. They continue on a little further, a little more cautiously, and they notice this object is growing in size. "What's that?" Josiah asks from behind Senora.

"It looks like a cluster of trees."

"Are you sure? It looks like it may be moving."

"No, it's not moving. It only looks like it is because we're moving," Senora says. They hear rumbling. "Is that rushing water? But I don't see anything resembling water." Josiah reaches out and grabs Senora's arm just before she falls off a cliff.

"Watch out," he yells. Before them stands a deep canyon. Far below they see a fast rushing river and a waterfall.

As Josiah pulls Senora back to a safer distance, she shivers from the cool breeze blowing up from the river. They can still see the sunbeams shining on the other side. "Jo, how are we going to make it across?" Josiah looks around and walks along the edge of the canyon. He soon sees a trail that leads down toward the waterfall. He motions for Senora to come over, and he points at the trail. Senora nods and they make their descent. The trail is steep and lined with needle trees. Josiah can see the river come into sight. As they reach the water's edge, he looks up and down the river.

"The river is flowing quite fast here. I think we should follow it and see if it might narrow farther downstream," He says. Senora adjusts the backpack straps on her shoulders and follows her brother. The river is still rushing fast, but it starts to widen. Senora puts her hand on Josiah's shoulder and points ahead of him. A fallen tree rests across a smaller part of the river.

"Look there," she says. "Do you think we can cross on that?" Josiah looks around at the surrounding trees, the fallen tree, and the rushing river.

"If we take it slow, we might be able. I don't see any other way across." He shrugs. Senora carefully climbs on top of the fallen tree. "Remember, don't look down," Josiah says to warn her.

She focuses on the other side of the river, holds her arms straight out on either side of her for balance, breathes in deeply, and takes her first step. With each small step she is reminded that she is not alone, and that the Lord is with her. "Therefore, since we are surrounded by so great a cloud of witnesses, let us also lay aside every weight." Senora stops. She removes the backpack from her back and tosses it to the other side. She regains her balance and takes another small step. "Then you will walk on your way securely, and your foot will not stumble.[65]" Senora finishes quoting the verse as she steps off the fallen tree on the other side. She turns to look at her brother. "Ok, Jo. Your turn."

Josiah swallows hard and nods. He climbs up onto the fallen tree. Straightening his arms out on either side, he finds his balance. He fixes his eyes on Senora and takes his first step. "God is our fortress and strength, a very present help

---

[65] Proverbs 3:23

in trouble. Therefore, we will not fear though the earth gives way, though the mountains be moved in to the heart of the sea, though its waters roar and foam." Josiah looks down at the rushing water below him. He sways a little but regains his balance.

"You can do this, Jo. Be brave and never give up." Senora says to reassure him.

Josiah takes a few deep breaths to compose himself and another step. "Though the mountains tremble at its swelling, there is a river whose streams make glad the city of God, the holy habitation of the most high God is in the midst of her; she shall not be moved; God will help her when morning dawns.[66]" Josiah loses his balance once more and starts to fall. Senora reaches out her hand and catches him. She pulls him to the river's bank. "Thanks," Josiah says, panting.

They stand up and turn to face a steep hill. Senora groans as she pulls the backpack back onto her shoulders; Josiah puts his hand on her shoulder. "It's ok, Nora. God's with us. He'll give us the strength we need." She smiles and nods. Josiah pulls out his shoelace and carabineer.

"Wait, Jo. I think we might have some rope in the backpack." Josiah nods, puts his shoelace back in his pocket, and reaches into the backpack to pull out a long climbing rope. "Here, this should help secure our footing and make the climb easier," Josiah says to reassure his sister. He bends down and re-laces his shoe to make his footing more secure. Josiah feels a rush of adrenaline as he secures Senora's anchor. He reassures her as he begins his own assent with a smile. He pauses every few minutes to secure a new anchor and connect the rope. Once he reaches the top, he turns and sets his position. "Ok, Nora, the anchors are secure." He tosses the other end of the rope down to Senora. She secures the end of the rope to her

---

[66] Psalm 46:1-5

carabineer and harness. Beginning her climb, Josiah carefully positions himself to protect his sister so she doesn't fall. Once Senora comes into view, Josiah pulls her to safety and wipes the sweat from his brow. Shaking with adrenaline, he turns to Senora. "Nora, are you ok?"

Panting for breath she turns to her brother with a big grin on her face. "That was awesome. Scary, but awesome. You learned how to do this at camp?"

"Yeah," Josiah says.

"No questions asked-I'm going to camp with you next year." Senora playfully punches Josiah's arm. Senora points at a cluster of trees ahead and they see the Red Dragon circling above them.

She turns to look at Josiah and adjusts the backpack. "Jo, can we rest for a bit? I'm thirsty." Josiah nods, and she pulls the backpack off once more, kneeling to open it. She pulls out the two water bottles and hands one to her brother.

Josiah takes the water bottle and sits down beside Senora. She hears some mumbling coming from down in the canyon. She quickly puts her water bottle back into the backpack and crawls to the edge, peering down the hill.

"What is it?" Josiah whispers. Senora can see movement; she soon realizes it's those men tracking them.

"Ok, where'd they go?" Lucas asks. "I see footprints up to here."

"I don't know, sir."

"Well, you better find the trail again. They couldn't have vanished," Lucas yells. Senora crawls away and rushes over to Josiah.

"We need to move. Those men are tracking us somehow. It won't take them long before they discover we crossed the river." She grabs Josiah's arm and pulls him to his feet. They start running towards the patch of trees in the distance.

CHAPTER 10

The Forgetful Woods

As they get closer to the trees, the wind starts to blow. Soon, the ground gets crunchy and turns to snow. Senora bundles up her coat, while Josiah quickly pulls one of the blankets out of the backpack and wraps it around his shoulders, while he continues to run. Josiah looks over at Senora and realizes her lips are turning blue and her tears are freezing on her cheeks. "You alright?" Josiah asks her.

"I'm a little cold, but I'll be ok," Senora says as her teeth chatter. Josiah reaches into the backpack and pulls out the other blanket, enveloping Senora's shoulders. "Thanks," Senora replies as she looks around. Feeling weak, she struggles to keep going, her knees give way losing her balance, and she falls on the snow-covered ground. Josiah runs to her side.

"Nora!" He notices that her hair is forming ice crystals. "Nora, talk to me."

She shivers and coughs. "Jo, I'm so cold." He rubs his hands over her arms, trying to warm her. Slowly, her hair starts to thaw, and the colour returns to her lips.

"Nora, what's going on?"

"I don't know. As we entered the forest, I suddenly got really tired and cold. I don't want you to get cold too."

"I'll be fine," he reassures her. They sit in the snow surrounded by many leafy trees. Most of the trees have lost their leaves, and the bare branches are swaying as if dancing to music.

She smiles at Josiah as she feels her arms warming up under the blanket. "Jo, I recognize this forest. I think this is where I was when I saw that girl skating. I think this might be the Forgetful Woods." Senora jumps to her feet excitedly as the wind carries her last words away.

"Ok, so where is this girl you mentioned? Right now, I only see us." Josiah looks around and kicks some snow off his foot. Soon, they hear singing, faintly at first, but gradually the song seems to grow louder as if it's being carried to their ears on the wings of angels.

Senora recognizes the tune from when she first started this journey. "Do you hear that, Jo? It's her. I just know it." Senora takes off running.

Josiah nods and runs to catch up to her. They slow their pace to a walk as Senora leads the way. In the distance, Senora recognizes the small hill. She looks over, and she sees movement ahead. "It's her," Senora says. Josiah looks over the hill beside his sister; he can see a girl skating on a small skating rink. This girl is tall, slender, with long auburn hair. Her movements are smooth as silk and swift as an eagle in flight. She glides along the ice. "Do you think that's the princess Lucas was referring to?" he asks.

"I don't know. Should we try talking to her?"

"We can try."

"Yes, remember when Lucas was talking on the phone? He said she was skating?" Senora reminds him. They cautiously approach the edge of the skating rink. "Hello?" Senora says. The girl continues to skate and sing. She starts to spin in a circle. The wind blows wildly, and as the girl spins, Senora can feel the chill of the wind cut right through her blanket. She shivers and falls to her knees. Josiah kneels beside her and hugs her to try to keep her warm. "Jo, she doesn't seem to notice us," Senora says through chattering teeth. "Wait, didn't Lucas also say that she would not wake up?" Josiah's eyes get wide as he remembers this too. "Maybe she's under a spell or something."

He notices the wind die down again as the girl starts skating smoothly in big figure eights, and her song becomes melodious and calming. His courage returns, and he looks at his sister shivering in his arms. "Nora, if we work together and trust God, we can save her. With man, this is impossible, but with God, all things are possible.[67]" Senora nods. She looks at the girl as she continuously skates and sings.

"But how are we going get her attention?" Senora can hear her own doubt with every word as she is almost spitting them out of her mouth through her chattering teeth.

"Let's pray, Nora. There's power in prayer," Josiah says to reassure her. They grab each other's hands and face one another. "Dear Heavenly Father, we know you are holy and all knowing. You are the King of kings, the first and last, beginning and end. You are all-powerful, and nothing is too difficult for You," Josiah prays.

"Lord, You are the Prince of peace, my Saviour and my friend. I'm unworthy to be called your child."

"Father, we need Your help, we cannot do this on our own." The wind starts to blow harder, Senora wavers, but Josiah clings strongly to her hands. He won't let her go. Not this time.

"Lord Jesus, You tell us that in our weakness Your strength will shine through." The ground shakes.

---

[67] Matthew 19:26

"You remind us that nothing is impossible for You. Your burden is light. You give ear to our prayers." The snow starts to fall from the branches almost cutting into their faces.

"God help us now. In Your power, You have all authority and all wisdom. Please grant us wisdom now."

"Let the wise hear and increase in learning, and the one who understands obtain guidance, to understand a proverb and a saying, the words of the wise and their riddles,[68]" Josiah says.

"Please show Your power. You have risen. You have won."

"Incline your ear, and hear the words of the wise, and apply your heart to my knowledge, for it will be pleasant if you keep them within you, if all of them are ready on your lips.[69]" Senora proclaims, "For I want you to know how great a struggle I have for you, that their hearts may be encouraged, being knit together in love, to reach all the riches of full assurance of understanding and the knowledge of God's mystery, which is Christ, in whom are hidden all the treasures of wisdom and knowledge.[70]"

"Father, you know our fears, our transgressions, and yes, even our doubts. Show us your power and authority now."

"Blessed is the one who fears the Lord always, but whoever hardens his heart will fall into calamity.[71]" The wind and snow blow so loudly that Senora can hardly hear her own words coming out of her mouth. "Please, Father, help us to save her."

"I praise you, for I am fearfully and wonderfully made. Wonderful are your works; my soul knows it very well.[72]"

"You know our every thought before we say them; you know our strengths and our weaknesses. You know our mistakes and our sins. Yet you still love us. Your thoughts of us

---

[68] Proverbs 1:5-6
[69] Proverbs 22:17-18
[70] Colossians 1:1a, 2-3
[71] Proverbs 28:14
[72] Psalm 139:14

outnumber the grains of sand in the entire world. I know I don't always come to you first, forgive me for this, but I pray you will hear me now. Show us the way, may your power shine through all the chaos and noise. You have the authority here and no one else."

When they feel they have no more strength, the wind suddenly stops, and all becomes calm. They both pray, "Amen." Senora can feel her arms tingle as they start to warm. She's the first to lift her head and open her eyes. She looks out over Josiah's shoulder, and she sees the girl lying on the ice. Senora touches Josiah, and he turns to look.

He gasps. "Quick. We need to get her off the ice," Josiah says to Senora, and they both walk toward the girl. They each grab an arm and pull her to the edge. Josiah removes her skates, and Senora checks her pulse.

The girl lies there lifeless. Her skin is rosy. "She's alive," Senora says, relieved. The girl's arms are cold and limp as she lies peacefully on the snow.

"Please wake up," Josiah says. Senora holds her hand and touches her forehead.

"She's breathing, but she feels very cold." Senora pulls the blanket off her shoulders and places it on the girl while Josiah does the same.

The two look over her for what seems like hours. The snow starts to melt and the fragrance of spring enters the air. In the distance, Senora can hear the roar of the Red Dragon. "Please wake up. Please God show us what to do," Senora prays as she looks up to the clouds.

The girl starts to cough and opens her eyes. Senora props up her head as Josiah hands her a bottle of water. Senora gives her a little drink.

"Thank you," the girl says hoarsely. She coughs again.

"Who are you?" Josiah asks the girl. The girl finds the strength to sit up. She takes another drink of water.

"I'm Princess Delores. Who are you?" she asks.

"I'm Nora, and this is my brother, Jo."

"We found you skating. You were singing a tune, almost like you were in a dream," Josiah says. Delores' eyes widen.

"I remember walking in the Forgetful Wood. I met a lady," Delores tries to remember.

"What did the lady look like?" Senora asks.

Delores says, "She was tall with long blonde hair, ruby red lips, emerald green eyes, and a lovely smile." Delores remembers. "Wait. No. It was not her. At least, I don't think it was her."

"Who?" Senora is puzzled and curious as to whom Delores is referring to. Is this the mysterious boss Lucas has been talking to and about, or is this someone new? Her head spins with questions and excitement all at the same time.

"I'm sure I'm not remembering right. We're friends. At least, I think we are."

"Who?" Josiah joins in the confusion.

"I'm sorry. My mind's foggy, and I'm not sure if I'm remembering correctly. But the one I am remembering is the queen."

"The queen? You mean your mother?"

"No, she's my aunt. But we have always been like sisters." Soon they hear breaking of branches. They look and see the Red Dragon walking towards them. Delores stands up. "Oh, Sam," Delores calls the dragon to herself. "I am so glad you're safe."

"You know this red dragon?" Josiah asks.

"Her name is Sam. She protects my kingdom."

"Wait. Did you say, *Sam*?" The Red Dragon nods its head and begins to transform. Its horns start to flow like fiery red hair, her emerald green eyes glisten, and soon Senora finds herself looking into the eyes of her friend Samantha.

"Delores, I'm glad you're safe. You've been under that spell for a long time," Samantha warns.

"Tell me, Sam. What have I missed?"

"The queen has taken over. She's hungry with power. She'll stop at nothing to stop anyone who she thinks will pose a threat," Samantha gives Delores a recap.

"Ok, then we need a plan to stop her," Delores says.

"Wait, I'm confused," Senora says.

"Sorry, let me explain. You see, long ago during the great battle with the Queen of the Dragons. Lucas was their King. He promised that the Silver Dragon and he would be eternally bonded. But when we vanquished the Dragon Queen, Lucas was outraged," Delores says.

"All the dragons went into hiding, and Lucas fell into the shadows. No one has heard from him in over 60 years," Samantha says.

"Honestly, I thought he killed himself with grief," Delores says, sadly.

"We aren't so lucky. He's back and he seems to have the Queen's ear," Samantha says.

"Wait. How is this possible if Lucas was the Queens enemy?" Josiah asks.

"That is what I intend to find out," Delores says.

"I'll keep watch from above. Nora, Jo, you can trust Delores." She transforms back into the Red Dragon, spreads out her large red wings, and flies off into the sky.

"She'll guard us from above," Delores says. "Now we need to make our way to the castle." Delores stands and walks over to a nearby tree where she reaches down and grabs a pair of boots that she puts on her feet. They put the blankets back in the backpack, and Josiah puts the backpack on his back.

"Wait. Did you say castle?" Josiah asks. "We just saved you, and now you want to go on a quest to find a castle?"

"Not find the castle. But save it. I'm sure there's more to this mystery than what you know and what I remember. We need to discover the truth."

"I was told that we need to discover what the Greatest Treasure is. Do you know what that means?"

"I'm sure the answers can be found at the castle," Delores says to reassure them both. She stands up, brushes some dirt off her knees, and turns to lead the way.

Senora smiles and places her hand on Josiah's shoulder. "Remember, Sam is my friend too. What better place to look for the Greatest Treasure, than to go to a castle? She just said she wants to find the truth. I say we go. Are you with me?"

Josiah has so many unanswered questions racing through his mind. *I just got Senora back*, he thinks. Is this going to be another trap like Scarlett's party? He knows Senora loves a good adventure, but he wouldn't forgive himself if anything bad happened to her. "Jo…" He's startled to hear his name, and he looks around to see who's calling him. He catches a glimpse of the tall, bearded man once again out of the corner of his eye.

What do I do? He wonders.

"When you pass through the waters, I will be with you,[73]" Josiah hears the words whispered in his ear.

Josiah looks from Senora to Delores and then to the man. Senora looks at Josiah expectantly, waiting for his answer. Will he come with her and Delores? Josiah wonders if the girls can even see the man standing there or not. "Be of good courage, and do not be afraid. He will not leave you or forsake you[74]."

"Jo?" He's startled out of his own thoughts when he hears Senora call his name again. "Are you alright? You seem lost in thought. Do you think we should go?"

Josiah looks at Senora and whispers the words, "Can we trust her?"

"If we put our trust in the Lord, then He will let us know somehow if this is the right thing to do or the wrong one. Right?" Josiah thinks about the new found wisdom of his little sister's words.

---

[73] Isaiah 43:2
[74] 1 Chronicles 28:20b

"I think you're right, Nora." Josiah turns to look at Delores. "Ok, you lead the way." Delores kneels and listens to the ground. "What are we listening for?" Senora whispers.

"I want to make sure the path before us is clear, so I was listening for any dangers ahead. Josiah and Senora kneel beside Delores and listen intently. They hear Sam flying above, the wind is slightly blowing, but everything else is quiet. Delores stands again. "All seems quiet." They cautiously move through the trees away from the melting ice on a small pond.

PART 4

Doubts Of Fear

CHAPTER 11

Chambers of Freedom

Delores leads them down a rocky road and around a corner. She stops and turns toward them. "We're too exposed here. Quick. In there," she says. The three of them run down into a ditch and up the other side into another set of trees. "Ok, we need to find a safe way to the castle."

Senora thinks about her own journey and the places she's been, and she remembers, *Well, my journey started here.* She asks, "Delores, are we near the Hills of Courage?"

"Yes, they're just over that hill. Why do you ask?" Delores asks.

"There is a tunnel where I hid."

Delores' eyes widen. "You found the Silver Tunnel? How? Nobody ever finds it, at least not unless they know where it is."

"Ummm, it may sound silly, but while running through the Hills of Courage, I was almost pushed to where the tunnel was. I think that maybe Sam showed me?"

"We're not alone," Josiah says, "The Saviour is guiding us."

"You know the Saviour?" Delores asks Josiah.

"Yes. He's Christ Jesus," Senora says.

"He loves us, and He died and rose again to defeat death. He lives and forgives. His death has saved us all because the price of sinning is death. His death has brought us life, and we only need to believe and trust Him," Josiah says.

"Wow, you both are wise for your ages; I didn't discover that until I was older. But I lost my way. Skating became more important to me. It became all I thought about," Delores says. "I thank God for reminding me of true salvation. Now, Nora, show me the way to the Silver Tunnel."

Senora nods, and they run across the gravel road again and into the field, up over the next hill. She can see many rolling hills and patches of trees. She points towards a barb wire fence. "That way." The three run down the hill and make their way toward the fence.

As they near the fence, Senora turns. "It's near there." She points at the barb wire fence, and they see a small hole or dip in the ground. Senora jumps down into the dip first and disappears. Delores and Josiah stop. Soon, they see Senora look up at them. "Come, I found the entrance." Senora says.

Once they are safely in the tunnel, Delores turns toward Senora and says, "It amazes me that you found this tunnel. I searched for this for years. It is a shortcut to my castle. My father used it in his first battle with the Dragon Queen. It provided a way out of the castle unseen and for his troops to ambush the Dragon's army from behind, but its path became lost to us over the years. Thank you."

"You're welcome, but where do we go from here?" Senora asks.

"Follow me," Delores says as they make their way through the tunnel. Senora recognizes the patch of trees on the other side, shivers at the thought of the fog, Robert, and Trevor.

"We don't have to go through the Field of Despair, do we?" Senora says.

Delores stops and, turns to face Senora with concern in her eyes. "No, when my father told me about the tunnel, he said that is was west of the castle, so we need to turn and head that way. My castle is just through those trees." Delores says to reassure Senora. Senora sighs in relief.

Josiah's jaw drops at the sight of Delores' castle as it comes majestically into view. It stands alone on top of a high hill, made of stone, about ten-story high, and has a view of everything.

The stone wall engulfs the castle, making it appear one with the mountain. There's a narrow stone bridge that leads to a large oval gate. On the other side, the castle falls away with a steep cliff. Josiah hears rushing water, and he looks down the cliff, where he sees a waterfall and a river flowing out the bottom. Small evergreen trees grow tightly together along each side of the river like the trees are forming a framework around it.

While Josiah is taking in the magnificent sight, he realizes the only way to enter this castle is through the oval gate. "How are we going to get in without being seen?" he asks.

"No worries. I know a way," Delores smiles. They turn and make their way to the bottom of the cliff. Josiah is amazed at the sight of the mountains and cliffs, which were hidden from sight when they were on the other side. Delores leads them to a small trickling river that flows out of a large rock tunnel. When they enter, it is damp, dark, and cold. Delores reaches down and picks up three long pieces of wood, walks over to pull out one of the blankets from the backpack, and tears three strips off it. She wraps the strips around the end of each stick. "Got a light?" Delores asks.

"Well, actually." Senora pulls out two flashlights, and Josiah takes his flashlight from his belt loop. "Will these help?"

"What? Why didn't you mention those sooner? I wouldn't have ripped the blanket." Senora chuckles at Delores as she hands her one of the flashlights and turns them on. "Ok, now that we have established a way to see, let's go." Delores leads.

They move slowly through the tunnel. The farther away from the entrance they move the darker and colder it gets. The ground is slippery from the water. They try to be careful where they place each step because there are holes in the rock floor where water has broken away the ground. Moving down hill, they seem to be heading farther into the mountain face. When it seems like they have been walking for hours, Senora finally sees a small light appear ahead of them.

Delores leads them toward the small light. They find themselves standing in front of an old wooden door. Josiah tries to open it, but it will not budge. "Locked." He sighs, "Now what?"

Delores puts her hand on his shoulder "It will be alright, Jo. Be brave. There is a password." She smiles and turns toward Senora. "Do you remember what Sam told you?"

She thinks for a while but also knows that she doesn't want to make the long walk back through that cold dark tunnel again, so she nods. "You mean, friendship is a bond, but family is unbreakable?" she asks. The door creaks a little. Josiah jumps and looks at the door.

"Ummmm, what just happened?" he asks.

Delores smiles, "She said the password." Josiah tries the door again. Still locked.

"But if that was the password, why is it still locked?" Josiah asks.

"Jo, what is the main thing you have learned in your travels so far?" Delores asks.

He swallows hard and nods. "Never give up." The door cracks and creaks again. This time Josiah and Senora jump at the sound. Josiah tries the door again. "Nope. Still locked. Wait I also heard that you were the key," he says to Delores.

She smiles, "I am, but you two are as well." Delores walks toward the door. She reaches into her pocket and pulls out a crystalline stone. She presses it onto the side of the door. "He gives strength to the weak and power to the powerless, and all things are possible with God who gives us strength." The door creaks again and the latch on the door releases. Delores places the stone back in her pocket and opens the door. Light fills the tunnel. They all turn off their flashlights and walk through the newly open door.

Once their eyes adjust to the light, they find themselves at the bottom of a long staircase. Senora turns and asks Delores, "What does it mean? I was told that you were the key, but also that we have to find the Greatest Treasure. What is the Greatest Treasure?"

Delores looks surprised. "Have you not figured that out yet? In time. And when the time is right, you'll know." Delores smiles and starts to walk up the stairs. Josiah and Senora both look at each other, confused. They shrug and turn to follow Delores.

They move slowly up the stairs making every effort not to make a sound. Delores stops so suddenly that Senora almost bumps into her and loses her balance. Senora falls backward, but Josiah reaches out his hands to stabilize her. She turns to look at Josiah after regaining her balance and mouths the words "Thank-you." Josiah nods as if to say *you're welcome*.

Delores turns her head, and says, "We're almost to the top of the stairs. At the top, is a long hallway. When I run, you all need to run right with me to the first door. Be careful not to be seen," Delores whispers the instructions. They take three more steps up the stairs and take off running. Within seconds, they are all safely in a bedroom, behind a closed door.

Josiah looks around the room. He can see a large king-size bed against one wall. The bed has a beautiful blue comforter draped over it, and the frame is dark wood with rod iron on the head. There are horse pictures on the wall, two side closets on the left of the bed, and a window with drawn brown curtains to the right. Delores turns to face the two closet doors, and she walks up to a poem hanging on the wall between the two closet doors.

"What do we do now?" Josiah asks. "The only way out of this room that I can see is the way we came in."

Delores smiles. "Things aren't always as they seem." She touches the bottom corner of the hanging poem. Josiah hears creaking. Delores smiles at him. "Let's go," she says as she steps into the farthest closet and disappears. Senora follows. Josiah walks over to the closet and steps in too. He finds the three of them standing in a small dark tunnel.

They walk up to another wooden door, and Delores leans her ear onto it to listen. All is quiet, so she slowly opens the door. The three walk into a giant room filled with what looks like tools and large equipment. Delores walks over to a set of metal shelves. She pulls out two swords and she hands them each to Josiah and Senora. "What are these for?" Senora asks.

"Just for protection. I hope that we'll not need them," Delores says to reassure her. "Listen, I have some friends who can help us. Last time we talked we made a plan for them to hide within the castle if I ever went missing. Take the secret passageway to the next door; you should be able to connect with them."

"But how will we know who they are?" Josiah asks.

"Well, if they shoot at you, it's not them." Delores laughs. "Just kidding. They will find you."

"Where are you going?" Senora asks.

"I'll meet up with you soon. I need to find something. I'll find you," Delores says as she disappears through the passageway.

"What was that all about?" Senora asks, confused.

"Not sure, but we should keep going," Josiah says. They both enter the secret passageway and walk toward the next door. Josiah slowly opens the door and peeks through. He can see a large kitchen with dark granite counters lined with many tan cupboards. Many different people walk around the kitchen busily.

Suddenly Senora grabs Josiah's arm, "Wait, Jo. Do you hear that?" Josiah closes the entrance and listens.

"What is that?" Josiah asks.

"I don't know, sounds almost like scratching or something. I think we should investigate." Senora says.

"You are always up for a new adventure. Haven't we had enough adventure for now?" Senora just waves off Josiah's question and starts walking down the passageway towards the sound. Scrape, scrape, soon they can here muffled voices. Senora finds herself up against a stone wall. She leans her ear on the wall to listen.

"Crystal, it's no use. You have been at that for hours. You know we won't be moved unless he allows it." Scrape, scrape. "Save you energy."

"Come on, Kat. He has kept us away for too long. I am tired of darkness. I want to see mom." Scrape, bang! "Wait, I think I broke something."

"I hope it wasn't your arm." Says the second voice. Senora can see a crack form in the wall. She knocks.

"Nora, what are you doing? We are not supposed to give away our location." Josiah says.

"Who's there? If you are here to help, kick the crack I made." The first voice says.

Senora looks over at Josiah. "What should we do?"

"Well, now they know we are here, find out who they are." Josiah says.

"You say first. Who are you?" Senora says.

"I only answer to Delores, and she is not here."

"Wait, did you say Delores?"

"Yeah, what's that to you?" The first voice says.

"We came with Delores. She has been freed from an enchantment." Senora says.

"An enchantment? Where is she?" the first voice says.

"Jo, help me pull away at the crack." Senora says. The two pull together, soon the wall falls away and as the dust clears Senora and Josiah peer in. They see two twin girls with long jet black hair and dark eyes. The one closest the wall is standing, covered in ash and dirt with her wrists chained together. The other girl is sitting with her back again the far wall and her wrists are chained to the wall. Josiah crawls through the hole and walks up to the second girl. He pulls out the sword Delores gave him and with the back end hits the chains to free her.

"How were you able to make that crack in the wall?" Senora asks.

"I used my surroundings. Just like Delores taught me. I put my hands together and started swinging the chain at the wall." the first girl says.

"How did you know it would work?" Senora says.

"I didn't, but he moves us every 5 days, so he doesn't raise suspicion." Says the second girl.

"Who do you mean?" Josiah says.

"Lucas, of course. Now I thought you said you came with Delores. Where is she?" the first girls say.

"She said she had to do something. But she had help within the castle. Would that be you?" Senora says.

Josiah and the second girl walk over to Senora and the first girl. "Ok, she will need us. I think I know where she would go." says the second girl.

"Wait, just a second." She pulls Josiah aside, out of earshot of these two girls. "Jo, we don't know anything about these two girls."

Josiah looks over his shoulder at the two girls and then back at Senora. "Your concerns are valid. But just think about it this way, we trust this princess Delores, and we know just about the same of her as we do of these two girls. How do we know that Delores is not leading us into a trap? She says this is her castle after all. Why are we sneaking in passageways?"

"You have a good point there. Ok, what do you suggest we do?"

"Well, throughout our journey so far we have both been told that we are to trust and work together." says Josiah.

"Right."

"I do also recall that we are to discover what the Greatest Treasure is."

"Right. But I'm still unclear as to what that is. Do you know or have any suggestions, Jo?"

Josiah scratches his head and thinks. The first girl clears her throat. "Well, are we ready to go?" she asks, impatiently.

"Nora, I don't think we have much choice here but to trust these two girls. Delores did mention that she had help. Maybe they're the help that she was talking about." Josiah turns around to face the two girls, looks over at Senora, and nods his head.

Senora nods back and looks past Josiah at the two girls. "Ok, lead on." Josiah walks over to the first girl and used his sword again to unlatch her chains as well. The two girls throw their chains on the floor and take off running down the passageway past many closed doors until they reach what seems like the end. Senora pauses when she hears Samantha's voice in her thoughts, *when you pass through the waters, I will be with you.*[75]

"Thanks for your gentle reminders, Sam. I appreciate it," Senora whispers.

She says a small prayer: "Thank you, Father, for being with me. Please give me wisdom and strength right now. Amen." The first girl leans on the door to listen. On the other side of the door, they can hear talking.

"So, you found a way to break free, did you? Well, you will never win, Delores." The queen laughs.

---

[75]   Isaiah 43:2

"What happened to you? We used to be friends," Delores says.

"Friends? Friends, you say?" The queen laughs again. "Maybe when I was young and naïve. I will take everything from you."

"But, I don't understand. Why?"

"You don't know?" the queen asks. "You took everything that was important to me."

"I don't understand. Why do you say that? Your friendship is a bond, and I care about you."

"Care? Do you even know the meaning of that word?"

"Please, help me understand! You were always so loving. Why so angry now?"

"Two words for you, Delores. Crystal and Katarina," the queen screams.

The two girls look shocked at each other as they continue to listen. Josiah and Senora are confused. Senora stands up and runs through the door with Josiah following. They stand next to Delores. Senora says, "Even though I walk through the valley of the shadow of death, I will fear no evil.[76]"

Josiah stands on the other side of Delores and says, "He gives strength to the weak and power to the powerless."

The queen is startled by their sudden appearance. "What is this? I should have known that you were a coward and that you wouldn't face me alone." The queen laughs. "You must be this Nora I have been hearing about. And…" She turns to face Josiah with a glamorous smirk on her face.

"Wait…Scarlett?" Josiah says. "What are you doing here?"

"Have you not figured that out yet? I'm the queen."

"Wait, Jo. Do you know her?"

"I had a run in with her before. Nora, be careful. Do not let her touch you."

---

[76] Psalm 23:4a

"Now, now, Jo. We mustn't give away all of our secrets." Scarlett laughs.

"Please know that God loves you, and He has a wonderful plan for your life," Senora says.

"Plan? A wonderful plan you say? My plans died when Delores betrayed me."

"How did she betray you?" Josiah asks.

"Why don't you ask her? She's the real enemy here. Not me." A tear falls down the queen's cheek. Senora's heart goes out toward the queen.

"The truth will set us all free," Senora says.

"I honestly don't know what you mean, Scarlett," Delores says.

"Liar! You stole them!" Scarlett screams.

"Who?" Delores asks. Scarlett moves toward Delores and swings a scepter at her. Delores falls to the floor. "Scarlett, I know you, and I never betrayed you." Delores looks up at Scarlett. Her cheek shows a trickle of blood on it.

"Lies! All you speak is lies." Scarlett yells, "I will end you." Senora and Josiah run to help Delores stand.

"Why does she think you betrayed her? Ask her," Senora says to Delores.

Delores finds the strength to speak, "Why do you think I betrayed you? What is wrong with Katarina and Crystal?"

Scarlett laughs again. "Do you not remember? You took them for a picnic. They were on the bridge." Scarlett shakes her head as her eyes fill with tears. "They're gone, and it's all your fault."

Scarlett raises her scepter again when Senora steps between them. "Who are Crystal and Katarina?"

"Ask her," Scarlett yells.

"Finally, be strong in the Lord and in the strength of His might,[77]" Senora gently tells Delores. "Put on the whole armour of God that you may be able to stand against the schemes of the

---

[77] Ephesians 6:10

devil. For we do not wrestle against flesh and blood, but against the rulers, against the authorities, against the cosmic powers over this present darkness, against the spiritual forces of evil in the heavenly places,[78]" Senora say to Delores to encourage her.

Josiah walks over to Delores and Senora. "Therefore, take up the whole armour of God that you may be able to withstand in the evil day, and having done all, to stand firm,[79]" Josiah calmly says to Senora.

"I never betrayed you. Katarina and Crystal are both safe."

"Lies. If they were safe then where have they been?" From behind Delores, the secret door creaks open. The two girls walk out and come to stand with Delores. "What? It cannot be. Kat? Crystal? Where have you been?"

Crystal speaks up. "We have been in the castle all this time, but Lucas has kept us away."

"You lie. Lucas has only my best interests at heart," Scarlett says.

"He knew we would threaten his hold on you," Crystal says.

"Hold on me? He has no hold on me. I hold all the power," Scarlett yells.

"But what has that power cost you?" Delores asks.

Katarina looks up and says, "You were right. We were on the bridge, but it wasn't Delores' fault we fell." She continues. "I was trying to be brave like you, and I dared Crystal to walk the rail. She slipped. I reached out to catch her, and we both fell off the bridge."

"But you're not hurt? Where have you been?" Scarlett asks.

"I know the girls liked to push themselves. You taught them to pursue greatness. I was trying to give them the freedom to explore. You always seemed to have them on such a tight leash. So many boundaries," Delores says.

---

[78] Ephesians 6:11-12
[79] Ephesians 6:13

"Boundaries kept them safe. Their teachers were to teach them greatness, not you," Scarlett says.

"I'm sorry I didn't watch them more closely," Delores says.

Katarina takes a deep breath and says, "I was scared to face you, scared to disappoint you. But then Delores disappeared. I tried to confront him, but he hid us away."

Crystals begs and says, "Please, Mom, let me tell you how we got on the bridge in the first place."

"I have heard enough," Scarlett yells.

"Lucas has shown me my true potential and the threat Delores was to my kingdom. So, I banned Delores to the Forgetful Wood," Scarlett says.

"I love you, Mom," Crystal says.

"How, after falling, are you not hurt?" Scarlett asks again.

"The Red Dragon. She saved us," Crystal says. Scarlett stiffens at these words. She steps back to look at both Crystal and Katarina.

"As I lost my grip and started to fall, the Red Dragon swooped down from the sky, caught us in her grip, and as she landed, wrapped us in a cocoon of protection with her wings. You see, we were under attack. While Delores was fighting off our attackers, we ran to the bridge," Katarina says.

"The Red Dragon, you say? She only brings destruction. She betrayed her own kind, and for what? Measly little humans? Love?"

"But Mom, I'm telling you the truth. She did save us. Listen to what you're saying. She chose a side and before, you commended her for it. What's changed?" Crystal asks.

"Mom, we speak the truth. We love you," Katarina says.

"Search your heart, Scarlett. You know what the truth is," Delores says to remind her.

Scarlett looks behind her toward the shadows. She smiles and says, "It's you who are trying to trick me. Don't be fooled. It's Delores who lies."

"But Mom. We're here. Delores didn't lie about that. Can't you see?" Katarina asks.

Senora notices movement again in the shadows behind Scarlett. She touches Delores' shoulder. "I think someone else is behind all of this. I keep seeing movement in the shadows just beyond my sight," she whispers in Delores' ear. Delores nods and looks at Queen Scarlett again.

"Scarlett, can you not see? Crystal and Kat are safe. They're right here. You can see clearly and hear their side of the story. I'm not lying to you."

Scarlett wavers a little. Her head starts to spin. She rubs her forehead. "Scarlett, please listen," Delores says.

"I…I…Delores lies…Crystal…Kat…I…I…Guards," Queen Scarlett yells, calling in her personal guards. Four men walk into the room.

"Yes, my queen," one of the guards answers.

Scarlett waves her hands toward Senora, Josiah, Katarina, Crystal, and Delores. "Take them away. I need to think."

"Mother, please. Why won't you listen?" Crystal says as the guards take her arm and pull her from the throne room. Senora walks out with the others, she looks over her shoulder, and sees someone move closer to Scarlett from the shadows, but she cannot quite make out who it is.

CHAPTER 12

The Battle Within

As the guards lead the group from the throne room, Katarina is fighting, kicking, and trying desperately to free herself from the guard's firm grip without success. Senora watches as the first guard opens a door. He pushes Crystal and Katarina into the room and shuts the door, locking it behind him. "Move," he says to the rest to continue down the hallway.

———◦◦◦———

Crystal falls to the floor on her knees as the guard pushes her into the bedroom. Katarina runs to her sister's side to help her stand. They hear the door being locked as the guard closes it behind him. "Are you ok, Crystal?" Katarina asks.

"I don't understand. Mom was not herself. I just don't understand, Kat." Crystal starts to cry.

The guard leads the group to the next door, pushes the other three into the room, and locks the door. Senora is confused and lost in her thoughts as to who she saw with Scarlett. She's pulled from her thoughts as she hears Delores and Josiah talking.

"What did the queen mean about your betrayal?" Josiah asks.

Delores hugs her knees as she sits on the end of the bed. "I don't know. She has changed so much. She's so angry. She wouldn't even listen to Kat. I'm confused myself. We used to be so close. I would have trusted Scarlett with my life."

Senora walks over to them. "What do we know so far?" she asks.

"The queen is not herself," Josiah says. "Plus, she has ulterior motives. I met Scarlett before."

"She thinks I betrayed her," Delores replies.

"Was your encounter with her before a good one, Jo?" Senora asks.

"I'm sorry to say, but no. She has a strong power."

"What do you mean strong power?" Delores speaks up.

"I don't understand it myself. She can find your greatest fears or desires and pull them to the surface."

"She never had that before," Delores says.

"You said that she wouldn't listen to Kat. Why is this significant?" Senora asks.

"Well, Kat and Crystal are her daughters. Scarlett loved both of them. Both Crystal and Kat were the world to her. She always used to listen to them."

"Maybe when she thought they were gone, grief took over. Grief has blinded her to seeing and understanding what truth is," Josiah says.

"Friendship is a bond, but family is unbreakable," Senora says. "God, our Saviour, is the most important thing. He binds us in the adopted family of God. God is the centre and definition of truth. Only through Jesus' sacrifice, do we have true life. I know what the Greatest Treasure is."

"But wait. Nora, there's more to this, that you don't know yet," Josiah says, interrupting Senora.

"What's that?" Senora asks. Suddenly, the door flies open, and the guards rush in. They grab Senora by the arms and remove her. Josiah runs at the door, but he's too late. The door slams shut and locks again.

"What will they do to her?" Josiah asks. "The Greatest Treasure is..." Josiah's words fade off, "God's love binds family together, and what God holds together, nothing can separate."

"Nora is a strong and wise young girl. If she believes as you do, she'll have the courage that God provides. She has the tools, now she needs to put them to the test."

"Test? What sort of test?" Scared, Josiah looks toward the door. "God, please protect Nora now and fill her mind with truth," he prays.

The guards lead Senora into a dark room and they sit her down in a chair. They leave the room and close the door behind them without saying a word. Senora sits in the dark room wondering why they didn't tie her to the chair. She walks to the door, but it's locked. Suddenly she's blinded by a bright light and Lucas' voice. "*Sit down*," Lucas yells. Senora stumbles back to the chair. The room goes dark again.

"What do you want?" Senora asks.

"Irrelevant," Lucas yells. "You're a bright young lady. You've a lot going for you. You like the easy road. Don't you?"

Senora swallows hard. She remembers many times where she had chosen the easier route. "The way is hard and narrow, the path to life, and it is few who find it," Senora says.

"I offer you freedom, treasure, power. You could even have the kingdom if you give me what I want," Lucas says.

"We store up treasure in heaven where moths cannot destroy it, and no one can break in and steal."

"Your heart lies to you," Lucas says.

"Where your treasure is, that is where your heart will be also."

Lucas growls with anger and says, "I am offering you friendship, acceptance, and peace."

"The friendship of the Lord is for those who fear Him, and He makes known to them His covenant. My eyes are ever towards the Lord, for He will pluck my feet out of the net,[80]" Senora says.

Water splashes in Senora's face. She coughs and wipes her face with her sleeve. "What kind of friendship is based on fear?" Lucas asks.

"It's not fear as in intimidation or making one scared. It's fear in giving honour where it's due. God brings life. You bring lies and confusion," Senora yells.

"I think it's you who's confused," Lucas whispers.

"I'm not the one hiding in the shadows. Am I?" Senora says with confidence in her voice that she never knew she had. She hears the door open and close again. "Hello?" There is no answer. She's alone in the dark room again. Her eyes start to adjust to the darkness, but it appears that the only thing in the room with her is the chair she's sitting on. Senora is left in the room so long that she starts to get sleepy. Her head bobs a few times. Her eyes feel heavy and she tries desperately to stay awake.

Two guards burst into the room again. As one guard holds Josiah firmly, the other grabs Delores and they take them

---

[80]   Psalm 25:14-15

out of the room. "I said move," the guard say to Delores as the guard shoves her from behind. Delores falls forward a little but continues moving forward, looking downward the whole way.

The guards lead the two down the corridor, turn left, and lead them down another corridor. Josiah notices that this corridor is dimly lit, which makes it harder to see where they're going. "Wait," Josiah hears the first guard say again as he pulls out his keys. He hears the guard unlock another door. The door creaks as the guard opens it. "Now move," he says and Josiah feels the guard's hand grab his arm and pull him forward.

They enter yet another corridor, and this one is even darker than the last one. The floorboards beneath his feet creak with each step. The air smells stale, and his breath feels cold as he breathes in. He hears the door slam shut behind them as the guard continues to lead. Soon he's pulled to the right and almost pushed into another door. He falls forward as he loses his balance. The room he falls into is illuminated with light. His eyes sting as they try to adjust. Delores comes to his side. "Are you ok?"

Josiah nods yes as he hears the door close and lock. "Where are we now, Delores? Where did they put Nora? I just got her back and now she's gone again. Where are Crystal and Kat? Why do you think they left them together? And why are we together? I'm so confused."

"I think that's their plan. Confused gives them the advantage. You must be strong, Jo. I know that you will see Nora again."

Josiah slowly stands up and starts to pace. "Sit down, Jo. You're making me dizzy." Delores says. Josiah nervously sits on a chair next to Delores with his arms crossed in front of him.

"I'm sorry, Delores. I'm just so worried about Nora. She has been gone so long. It seems like I just found her only to lose her all over again." Josiah punches his fist on the chair, jumps up and starts pacing again.

"I know, but we need to think things through. Please, sit down. Nora was saying something before. Remember…about someone else in the throne room."

Josiah stops pacing again and looks at Delores. "You're right. I'm not helping Nora by pacing. We need to figure out this mystery." Josiah sits beside Delores again, a little calmer. "Tell me what you know about Queen Scarlett and about Crystal and Kat."

"Well, Scarlett, as you know, is my aunt. She has suffered lots. She lost her husband to a sickness. Her twin daughters, Crystal and Kat, helped her grieve and recover. I helped Scarlett raise the girls. But a few years ago, I remember her mentioning that she met someone. She said he was clever and wise."

"Do you remember meeting him or hearing a name?"

"I don't remember. I just know that meeting him made her very happy. But things changed." Delores shakes her head sadly.

"Changed how?"

"Well, she began to demand more and not waiting for a response. She began to make strange decisions and not listen to anyone's advice. When questioned, she'd get angry."

"What do we know about Crystal and Kat?"

"They're very close. Friendship and family are very important. They also mean the world to Scarlett, at least they used to," Delores says.

"So, if she thought something bad had happened to them, what would happen?"

Delores' eyes widen, and she says, "She would do everything she could to protect them. If she thought they might be gone, it would destroy her."

"Do you think this other man may have known this? How is the best way to destroy and gain control of someone or something?"

"You would want to destroy them and make yourself the one to save them."

"Do you think this man made Scarlett believe that you betrayed her, the Red Dragon killed her daughters, and he was the only comfort she would have? He would have control, and she would blindly trust only him." Josiah says in a shocked voice.

"But she has seen Crystal and Kat are safe," Delores says sadly to remind Josiah. "Why did she not see by that, who was the truthful one?"

"I don't know. I think there is something greater happening here that we just cannot see."

Delores puts her arm around Josiah's shoulders. "It's ok, Jo. We'll discover the truth. Why don't we pray?" The two bow their heads.

Crystal kicks at the locked door. "You let me out of here. I need to speak with my mom," she screams.

Katarina sits calmly on a chair next to a window and looks out to the sky. "Calm down, Crystal. You know that we will only see Mom if he allows it."

Crystal kicks the door again, turns, and stomps over to her sister. "I know, but if we don't make a stink, then we will never get out of here." Crystal looks at her sister and places her hands on her hips. "What are you looking at anyways?" she asks.

Katarina looks back at Crystal. "Oh, I was thinking about what mom said. You know about Delores betraying her. I know she didn't. You remember how we almost lost her after dad died?"

Crystal's arms fall to her sides, and she hangs her head sadly. "Yes, I remember, but we're still here."

"I know, but she's blinded by grief and she only sees what he tells her. We need to find a way to help mom see the truth. Sit with me; help me to find the answer." Crystal slumps down in the chair next to her sister and rests her chin in her hands with her elbows on the table. Katarina turns to look out the window again.

The two sit in silence for quite some time when they hear the door unlatch. They jump and turn to look. Queen Scarlett enters the room. The girls stand up and run toward her to give her a hug. But just before they reach her, they both stop.

"Who are you?" Scarlett asks.

"Mom, it's us. You know, Kat and Crystal." Tears well up in Crystal's eyes.

"Mom?" Katarina walks slowly up to Scarlett. Scarlett steps back, looking confused. "Mom, it's me."

Queen Scarlett rubs her forehead. "I...I don't know. But Delores..."

"Delores is your niece. Mom, please remember," Katarina says.

"Delores betrayed me. She and that beast."

"No, Mom. Please listen. The Red Dragon saved us. We're safe, can't you see?"

"Kat, what's wrong with Mom?" Crystal asks with fear in her voice.

Katarina steps closer to Queen Scarlett. The queen holds up her hand to stop her. "Stop," she yells. "You can't be her."

Crystal pushes past Katarina and hugs Scarlett tightly. "Mom, please remember! I love you!"

Queen Scarlett hugs Crystal back and starts to understand but suddenly pushes Crystal away. "Enough. No tricks." She rubs her forehead again. "I cannot lose them all over again. It's just too painful."

Scarlett turns on her heels and leaves the room. The girls hear the door lock behind her again. "What's wrong with Mom?" Crystal asks Katarina.

"I don't know, but I bet you that he has something to do with it." Katarina turns and sits back in the chair and looks out the window again.

"He has kept us away ever since Delores went missing. Kat, what are we going to do?"

"We wait. All will be made clear in the right time," Katarina says to reassure her sister.

Crystal stomps one foot, returns to her chair next to Katarina, and rests her chin in her hand. "I hate waiting." She sighs.

Katarina smiles as she sees a familiar shadow move by the window. She jumps up and runs to the window sill. "Time to go, Crystal. Sam will help us. We'll find a way to save Mom, Delores, and the others." The Red Dragon flies close to the window and Katarina crawls out onto her back. Katarina holds out her hand to help her sister climb on too. The Red Dragon flies away from the window and down towards the hidden tunnel. The two girls slide off Sam. Katarina turns and waves as the Red Dragon transforms back into Sam. "Thank you." she yells.

"I am coming with you this time," Sam says.

"Ok, let's go." Katarina takes the lead, and the three girls enter the cave. As they make their way to the door, Katarina stops suddenly. "We don't have the crystal. How are we going to get in?"

Sam steps forward. "There is more than one way to open a door."

"Wait, there is not enough room in here for you to transform." Crystal says.

"I don't need to transform to use a little fire." Sam says with a smirk. She placed her hands on the door, her hands start to glow, as she removed her hands the door sparks and engulfs in flames. When the door falls forward to the ground the dust snuffs out the flames. "See, told ya. Now where are the others."

Crystal nods her head in surprise, "OK, then. That will do it. Let's just hope the guards didn't hear that." The girls cautiously step through the open doorway.

Senora is startled awake when she hears the door open and close again. "Who's there?" she whispers. She can hear someone walking around the room, and she can make out a person moving. "I can hear you," she says. The person continues to walk around the room, obviously staring at her. Senora shifts in her chair nervously. "Who's there?" she asks again.

"What's the matter, Nora? Afraid of a little silence?" Lucas asks. A cold shiver creeps down Senora's spine. "Why is that? Do you like to hear the sound of your own voice?"

"What? No, that's not it at all," Senora says.

"Silence. I'm the one asking the questions here," Lucas yells. The figure moves about the room quietly once again. Senora shifts nervously and swallows hard. "Nervous, Nora?"

"No. I just wish I knew what you wanted," Senora whispers. She can hear Lucas laughing. "Don't laugh at me," Senora yells.

"Good, good." Lucas claps his hands. "Feed your anger."

"Whoever is slow to anger has great understanding, but he who has a hasty temper exalts folly,[81]" Senora says.

Senora hears Lucas shuffle his feet and pace once more. "You deserve to have respect," Lucas says. "Take revenge on those who hurt you."

"Beloved, never avenge yourselves, but leave it to the wrath of God, for it is written, 'vengeance is mine, I will repay, says

---

[81] Proverbs 14:29

the Lord.'[82]" Senora says. She hears Lucas growl. She can see him stop and stare intently at her. Senora shifts again.

"What is it you want? I don't understand," Senora whispers.

"Silence," Lucas yells. Senora shivers. She hears the door open and close and she finds herself alone once more. Not too long later she hears the door open and close again.

"Who are you?" She's startled when she hears a gentle woman's voice. The light comes on in the room, and Senora squints as her eyes adjust to the light. Once her eyes refocus, there before her stands the queen. "Why are you here?" she calmly asks.

"I came to help my brother, Jo," she whispers. "We saved the princess."

"Princess? What do you mean?" Scarlett asks.

"Princess Delores."

"Delores? What does she have to do with this?"

"Don't you know? You saw Crystal and Kat." Senora looks up.

Scarlett rubs her forehead and shakes her head. "You are trying to trick me."

"Crystal and Kat. The ones you were talking to Delores about."

"I, I," Scarlett says, stumbling over her words.

"It's not a trick." Senora reaches out her hand and grabs hold of Scarlett's. "Friendship is a bond, but family is unbreakable."

Scarlett pulls her hand away and her eyes grow wide. "What did you just say?"

"Friendship is a bond. You know Delores is your friend. But family is unbreakable. Crystal and Kat are your family. Just like Jo is my family. Crystal and Kat are alive. You saw for yourself. Family is unbreakable. They love you, and that will never change," Senora says gently.

---

82   Romans 12:19

Scarlett kneels to look in Senora's eyes. "I thought they were dead."

Senora places her hand on Scarlett's shoulders. "You were deceived," Senora says.

Scarlett stands again. "Nora, don't lose heart. You have reminded me and my mind is finally clear. I thank you for that. Now I need to finalize some things. You stay here a little longer." She turns on her heels, turns off the light, and leaves the room. Senora is left alone in the dark room once more.

CHAPTER 13

The Power to Open the Truth Revealed in the Greatest Treasure

Sam, Crystal, and Katarina make their way up the stairs and run across the hallway. They unlock the door and enter the secret passageway. "Now girls, where would they keep Delores, Nora, and Jo?" Sam asks.

Katarina tries to think "Kat, are you with me?" Sam asks.

"Yes, sorry. There's an old part of the castle, one where dad and mom had their happy times, before he got sick. She might have taken them there. You know away from any listening or questioning ears."

"Ok, can we get to that part of the castle through these passageways?"

"It will be difficult to remember, but there is a way. I will try." Crystal turns to the right and the girls run down a dark tunnel. She stops at a small panel in the wall of the tunnel, pushing on it and sliding it open. The fragrance of mould, dust, and moth balls reach their noses.

"What's that smell?" Sam coughs.

"I know it's unpleasant, but it's the only way. You're not afraid of spiders, are you?" Katarina asks. Sam looks into the new tunnel, and it's full of cobwebs.

"Let's go. Lead the way." The girls push their way through the cobwebs until they reach a dead end. "Now where?" Crystal leans back and starts kicking the wall.

"She had this part of the castle sealed off after Dad died." Crystal kicks again. Suddenly, her foot breaks through. Sam crawls up beside her and starts pushing and pulling to make the new hole wide enough for them to fit through. Once they stand up and brush the remaining cobwebs off, Sam looks around; they're in a dimly lit corridor.

"Delores, are you here? Jo, Nora. Can you hear me?" Kat yells. They make their way down the corridor stopping at each set of doors and call out again.

Soon Delores hears Sam's voice. She jumps and runs to the door knocking on it. "In here. I'm in here. Sam, is that you?"

Sam pauses at the door when she hears Delores' voice. "Kat, Crystal, wait. I hear Delores."

Delores knocks again. Sam, Crystal, and Katarina run past three more doors to where the knocking is coming from. Delores is startled to hear Sam, Crystal, and Katarina banging on the door. "Stand away from the door." Sam says. Delores steps away and stands next to Josiah. Bang! The door falls in. Sam is standing there with Katarina and Crystal.

"How did you?" Delores says.

"She used her surroundings." Crystal says.

"No, I just kicked down the door." Sam says.

Delores hugs them. "Sam, what are you doing here? Kat and Crystal, I am so thankful you're safe."

"Delores, Mom came to see us, but it was as if she didn't even know us," Katarina says.

"I think she's confused somehow," Crystal says.

"There was someone else in the throne room," Josiah says.

"Do you think it was him?" Crystal asks nervously.

"It must be," Katarina answers.

"What? Who?" Delores asks.

"He has been deceiving all of us," Katarina says.

"Who's he?" Josiah asks. Soon two guards approach the newly fallen door.

"How did you three get here?" one guard asks. Josiah runs toward the two guards and spins his leg into a high kick, knocking the first guard out. "You little!" Katarina hits the second guard in the head with a vase, and he falls with a thud.

"I need to find my sister. Remember, friendship is a bond, but family is unbreakable," Josiah says. He looks through the guards pockets and pulls out a crumpled piece of paper. He slowly unravels it. He reads: *Senora is the key and she must not stay with Josiah. Senora knows what the Greatest Treasure is. Never shall the two be left alone.*

Josiah's eyes widen as he looks up at Delores. "We have work to do. We've presented the truth to Scarlett."

"We need to know what we're dealing with." Delores turns to look at Katarina. "We first need to get to the secret tunnel and find Nora." She looks at Josiah. "Did you find anything else?" Josiah looks in the other guard's pockets. He pulls out a necklace that looks like a silver eagle. "I thought that was lost," Delores says.

"This pendant, I remember it. Nora had it when we...." Josiah's words fade off.

"It's Queen Scarlett's signet pendant. She uses this to pass law and to show her rule. But why would this guard have it?" Katarina asks. "Mom never would take it off. Unless..."

"Before these guards wake up, we need to move. We can discuss this when we're safe," Delores says. She leads all of them quietly out of the room and down a long hallway. They enter another room which looks like an office full of three desks. Delores walks over to a fire truck clock hanging on the wall; she pulls gently on one of the hanging cords. They hear a door open. Delores kneels and crawls under a nearby desk. She calls over her shoulder, "follow me." They each follow Delores into a new passageway, one by one. Josiah is the last one to crawl through and once the door closes behind him, Delores whispers, "Ok, we're safe for now."

Josiah looks at Delores. "So, what's the deal with this necklace? And why did that note say that Nora knew what the Greatest Treasure is? How would they know?" he says.

"First, let's see if we can find Nora. Then, we can discuss everything else."

Josiah nods. "So, where would they have taken her?"

"Probably the interrogation room," Crystal replies. Delores agrees and leads the way.

"How do you know your way around these tunnels so well?" Josiah asks. Delores looks over her shoulder and smiles.

"Because I grew up in the castle. When I was a kid, I would play tricks on the guards and hide in here. After a while, the path became second nature."

"And the guards never found out about these tunnels?"

"Nope. The only ones who know about these are all who are here now and Nora." The group slowly and quietly continues. *This is definitely smaller than the other secret passages*, Josiah thinks. It's dark, damp, and a little chilly. He shivers.

Delores stops suddenly and puts up her hand to quiet the others. Josiah can hear voices.

"Just relax. I'm here, and I'll keep you safe." Josiah recognizes the voice. It's Lucas. *But what is his role in all of this?* he wonders. "In time all will be made clear."

"I don't know what I would do without you," Scarlett says.

"Just rest now. I'll take care of everything. Here, take this drink, it will give you the clarity you seek. Don't worry about those children. They're nothing to you. I will deal with Nora. I told you that Delores was a traitor. She has just proved that with this group of rebels she so mysteriously showed up with," Lucas whispers.

"Thank you, Lucas. The truth is the only answers that I seek. Find that truth and report back to me." They hear a door close.

"But what truth does Scarlett seek? She seems confused somehow and what drink did Lucas give her?" Josiah asks.

Delores notices concern in Josiah and Sam's eyes. "We will figure something out. Let's keep going. We need to find Nora," Delores reassures them. They continue to crawl single file through the tunnel, and they stop suddenly when they hear more voices.

"What do you mean they're not in their room? And Delores? Jo? You're so incompetent." They can hear Lucas yelling, "Find them, or the queen will have your heads!" They hear people running and a few different "Yes sirs" in response. Suddenly, all goes quiet.

Delores looks over her shoulder. "We're almost to the interrogation room," she whispers to Josiah. Josiah responds with a nod. Delores turns a corner and crawls up to a grate. It's dark and quiet on the other side. They listen to make sure nobody is coming. Delores slowly pushes the grate open.

"Who's there?" Senora's says.

Delores walks close to Senora. "How are you?"

"I'm tired. Lucas has been trying to confuse me," Senora says. She sees Josiah from behind Delores. "Jo, are you alright?" she asks with concern in her voice.

"Delores, we need to get Nora out of here. I'm fine, Nora. How about yourself?" Josiah asks.

Senora nods weakly. "Stay strong, Nora," Delores says. "If he comes back, do you think you can record your conversation?" Delores hands Senora a recording device. "When he enters, push the record button."

"I don't know if he will be returning." Senora swallows hard.

"Can you please try, Nora? I will only ask this once then we will get you to safety." Delores reassures both of them. Senora nods. The rest re-enter the tunnel and close the grate behind them. Josiah can hear footsteps. These footsteps appear to be moving quickly and getting closer. They sit as quietly as they can and start to pray for Senora. They hear the door open and slam shut.

"So, Nora," Lucas says, "what are you waiting for? You're free to leave anytime. Nobody's stopping you."

Senora is confused by this change of conversation. "What do you mean?"

"What do I mean? The door's not locked; you're not tied to the chair. So, what's stopping you?" Lucas asks.

"Jo," Senora whispers.

"Now we're getting somewhere. Where is he, Nora? No harm will come to you. Just tell me where he is."

"Why? What do you want with him?"

"Have you not figured that out? You're good at lies. Lies protect you, don't they?" Lucas asks.

"What? No, I'm not," Senora says.

"Aww, did I hit a nerve? Search your heart. You will know it to be true."

"But the king shall rejoice in God; all who swear by Him shall exalt, for the mouths of liars will be stopped,[83]" Senora whispers.

"Stopped? Stopped you say?" Lucas laughs. He swings his fist at Senora's face, and Senora falls to the floor. "Not stopped. Lying is all around you. 'I said in my alarm, 'All mankind are liars,[84]" Lucas replies.

---

[83]   Psalm 63
[84]   Psalm 116:11

Senora staggers back onto her chair. "An evildoer listens to wicked lips, and a liar gives ear to a mischievous tongue,[85]" Senora says.

"What do you desire, Nora? Love? Gold? Money? Power? I can give all this to you and more."

"What is desired in a man is steadfast love, and a poor man is better than a liar.[86]" Senora looks up at Lucas, and she can see him pacing back and forth. "You are of your father, the devil, and your will is to do your father's desires. He was a murderer from the beginning, and does not stand in the truth, because there is no truth in him. When he lies, he speaks out of his own character, for he is a liar and the father of lies.[87]" Senora fills with confidence.

Lucas moves quickly behind Senora and comes right up to her ear. "Then, what does that say about you? I know how you really feel. Jo is not nice to you. Many times you have said you hated him. Just tell me where he is, and all will be good. You'll never have to see him again. You want this, don't you? I can even make you forget all the pain, trials, and hurt he has caused you."

Senora remembers many fights she and Josiah have had with each other, but she's also reminded of all the good times too. "Let God be true though everyone were a liar, as it is written, 'that you may be justified in your words, and prevail when you are judged,'[88]" Senora says, "If we say we have not sinned, we make Him a liar, and His word is not in us.[89]"

"What is sin? And what is truth?"

"Sin is everything that goes against God. Truth is what conforms to reality. A formal worldview based ultimately upon

---

[85] Proverbs 17:4
[86] Proverbs 19:22
[87] John 8:44
[88] Romans 3:4
[89] 1 John 1:10

that nature, character, and being of God as it is expressed in His infallible word, the Bible, and His creation. It becomes the foundation for a life system that governs every area of existence.[90]"

"Existence? Life system? What makes the Bible infallible?"

"The truth is God's truth, as set forth supremely and most definitively in the Bible and we regard this truth to be absolute in the sense that it cannot be compromised and it's not open to purely subjective interpretation. Ultimately, we cannot dissect the truth; we only proclaim it,[91]" Senora says.

"Proclaim it, you say? How?"

"By sharing the good news."

"Good news? What good news?"

"That sin separates us from God because He is holy and will not be around sin. But He sent His son, Jesus Christ, to come to the earth, He created."

"If He came, then where is He now?"

"You see, sin brings death. But God still loves us. Jesus is God and had no sin. So, He died and took that penalty of death and God's anger on Himself."

"So, God is dead."

"No, that is not the end. It's only the beginning. You see, we're walking in sin daily. It's all around us. Jesus loves us, and with His death, He set us free to be with God again."

"How can one set us free if He is dead?"

"But He's not dead. Three days later He came back to life and concurred sins hold on us. Freeing us for God's forgiveness and grace."

"What does it mean to forgive? And what is grace?"

"Forgiveness is when someone chooses to release feelings of resentment or vengeance towards a person or group of people

---

90   Focus on the family
91   The truth Project

who have hurt them, no matter what. Even if they actually deserve forgiveness or not. Grace is getting something even when you don't deserve it."

"Sounds like weakness," Lucas sneers.

"In my weakness, God's strength shines through. I'm not alone. God's with me." Senora sees Lucas lean against the door. She swallows hard and clears her throat. "But He said to me, 'My grace is sufficient for you, for my power is made perfect in weakness, so that the power of Christ may rest upon me.'[92]"

"Don't you lie, manipulate, and say mean words though? You're nowhere near perfect," Lucas says.

Senora squirms at these words, but she feels confidence grow within her once more. "For the sake of Christ, then, I am content with weakness, insults, hardships, persecutions, and calamities; for when I am weak, then I am strong.[93]"

Senora can see Lucas pacing again. "When you're weak you're strong? That sounds opposite. How can you boast about being weak? When someone is weak, they're easier to crush, easier to conquer." Lucas growls.

"No. Not true. When I feel alone, scared, tired, I just pray and rest in God's strength. He is stronger and more powerful than anything, and He can crush anything with just a breath. I trust in His truth and strength. I need Him. 'He created me, and I am his workmanship.' I choose to follow and walk in His forgiveness."

"But you still sin. You said God is holy. So, he cannot be around sin."

"Yes, but when God looks at me, He sees Jesus' perfection. Jesus is healing me, and no, I'm not perfect. I will never be perfect in this lifetime. Perfection comes with eternal redemption when I live with Christ for all eternity. I'm still learning

---

92   2 Corinthians 12:9
93   2 Corinthians 12:10

and growing. I make mistakes, but I can run into God's arms anytime and be forgiven and loved," Senora says.

Lucas groans. The door slams again. Josiah can hear the footsteps moving off into the distance. Delores pushes the grate open and walks over to Senora. Senora hands Delores back the recording device. "I'm not sure what you were looking for in the conversation but all our conversations have been like this one."

"You did great, Nora. Now let's go see Queen Scarlett."

"Queen Scarlett? She came to see me," Senora says.

"She did? What happened?"

"We talked about who I was. Why I was here. She seemed very lost and confused. At first anyway," Senora says.

"At first? What do you mean?" Delores asks.

"Well, I explained that friendship is a bond and how you cared about her. I reminded her of your friendship. Then, she asked about Kat and Crystal."

"What about them?"

"Scarlett did talk to us too. She seemed like she didn't believe we were who we said we are," Crystal says.

"She didn't at first. But I talked to her about how family is unbreakable." Senora looks at Josiah. "I explained how much Jo, my brother, meant to me. How I would do anything for him. I told her that Crystal and Kat were her family." She looks toward Crystal and Katarina and says, "Suddenly, she seemed to understand. She thanked me for helping her to see clearly. But She told me that she had to finalize some things and left."

"I wonder what she meant by 'finalize some things?' Katarina asks.

"I'm not sure. Sorry, that's all I know." Senora shakes her head.

"Ok, we should go," Deloris says.

"Go? Go where?" Senora is confused.

"It's time you and Jo stand up and use the Greatest Treasure. You two are the key."

"What?" Josiah looks at Senora. "Nora, what is the Greatest Treasure?"

"In time, you will see. Besides, I think you already know," Senora replies.

"Quick. It's not safe here. We must go," Delores says. All six of them climb back into the tunnel. Senora is the last to enter. She turns and pulls the grate back in place.

PART 5

From Confusion To Clarity

CHAPTER 14

Is death the end?

"Where are we headed, Delores?" Senora whispers.

"Back to the throne room to challenge Lucas," Delores says.

"I want some more answers regarding what happened to my mom," Katarina says.

"We all want answers," Delores says.

"I would like to know more about Lucas and this Silver Dragon," Josiah says.

"The Silver Dragon destroyed all the rest of the dragons. Lucas would gather them together, and she would absorb their energy. Each one she touched made her stronger." Sam says.

"Yes, but how was she defeated before?" Senora asks, determined to find some answers.

"The Saviour's words weakened her, and the more who believed, the weaker she got. If you believe in the Saviour, she cannot harm you. Eventually, Queen Scarlett entrapped her. At least, that's what I thought. Lucas went into hiding, the kingdom was safe, and the treasure was forgotten."

"The treasure. It's salvation, isn't it?" Senora asks.

"Yes, that's why you have the power within. You and Jo hold the good news within your souls. If he can break one of you, all will be lost," Sam replies as she looks over her shoulder. "A dragon has the ability to transfer one's conscience into another before they die, but she was defeated and banished. She didn't die," Sam says.

Delores leads them through the dark tunnel, until it comes to another opening. She pauses to listen and waves to quiet everyone.

"What is it, Delores?" Senora whispers.

"We need to be still. When we enter the next corridor, we need to be careful not to be seen re-entering the next passage way." They all nod in agreement. Delores mouths the words, one, two, and three. They all crawl out into the bright corridor and quietly shuffle down the hallway. "We are almost there," Delores tells them quietly. As they reach what looks like the end of the hallway, the door opens from behind them.

"Guards, I have a visual." The group runs to find a safe place to hide. Crystal moves swiftly and quietly out of sight to hide in the shadows. Katarina, Delores, and Senora run in the opposite direction toward an open door, and Josiah follows Sam back toward the previous tunnel. A group of guards meet in the corridor.

"I know they're here. Fan out and find them. Then, report back to me," the first guard orders.

Delores, Katarina, and Senora crouch quietly as they watch two guards approach their location.

"Nora, Kat, we're not far from the next passage way. When I give the order, we must run," Delores says.

"But what about the others?" Senora worries about her brother.

"I saw Jo with Sam. She knows the way. They can meet up with us. Crystal knows where to meet as well. Everything will be fine. Do you trust me?"

Senora shuffles her feet and nods. She looks as the two guards are almost to the point where they could see them. Delores and Katarina take off running, but Senora hesitates a little. "Now. Nora, Run," Delores yells over her shoulder.

"We have visual of three girls, in pursuit," one guard says into his walkie talkie. Delores and Katarina suddenly disappear from before Senora. She pauses to look around. Soon Senora feels Delores pulling her into the passageway. Once they are all in, Delores turns to look at her. "Are you alright?"

Senora nods and starts to speak when she's pulled away from Delores. Out into the hallway. "I told you I would always find you," Lucas yells into her ear and drags her away.

Delores sits in the passageway with her mind spinning. "What do I do now? I can't risk being exposed, not now. I will get you free, Nora, be strong," she whispers as she retreats further into the passageway with Katarina. "We must regroup with the others."

"Let go of me. What do you want with me?" Senora says.

"You still don't know?" Lucas laughs and drags her into an old dusty room one that has not been occupied for years. He throws her to the floor.

"I have never done anything to you."

"No, it's what you will do."

"What's that supposed to mean?"

"You pose a threat to my love and to my plan."

"Your love? Who's that?" Senora's mind starts to spin.

"The Silver Dragon. She has returned, thanks to me."

"What did you do to Scarlett?"

"I helped her discover her true potential." Lucas smirks. "At least, that's what she believes." Lucas chuckles as he leaves Senora alone in the room.

Lucas returns almost as quickly as he had left. "Now, since this will probably be your last day, I guess you can see." He pulls a small green flask from his pocket.

"What do you mean my last? What are you going to do?"

"To fully bring my love back, we need the Greatest Treasure destroyed."

"Why?"

"I started the process with Queen Scarlett. Slowly at first. I had to gain her trust. What better way than to remove the one thing she loved the most."

"What are you talking about? You say this flask contains the blood of the Silver Dragon?" Senora asks.

"After the final battle, she was defeated by the king and his forces. I knew." Lucas says.

"Knew what?" Senora says.

"I acted swiftly. With her final heartbeat, I took her last blood of life. You see, it is poisonous to men, but reacts differently in women. As the king breathed his last, I stepped in to bring Scarlett comfort. But those two girls of hers kept getting in the way. I had hidden Kat and Crystal from her and convinced her of Delores' betrayal." Lucas says.

"But why?" Senora says.

"I will do anything to bring my love back. I slowly introduced this elixir to the queen's diet. Soon, once we destroy the light altogether, Scarlett will be gone and only my love will remain."

"You're mad," Senora screams.

"Thank you for the compliment." Lucas bows toward Senora.

"What're you going to do with me?"

"You weren't part of the plan. I need to find something special for you. But for now, I need to go see my love. Until next time, enjoy your accommodations." Lucas says.

"Wait. I don't understand." Senora stands and looks around the room as Lucas closes the door behind him. She can see something hanging on the far wall. It appears to be an old painting covered in dust. She carefully brushes the dust away. It's a painting of the royal family. She can see Crystal and Katarina smile at a younger Scarlett. "She looks so happy here. No hatred in her eyes. *What did Lucas do to you?* She's shocked to see the face of the king. "The tall, bearded man? He's the king? But…"

"Yes, Nora." Senora jumps at the sound of her name from behind her. She slowly turns to see the tall bearded man standing before her. "I heard you were dead. How is this possible?"

"I'm only here in spirit. I'm here as a guide. I was the one who originally called you and Jo here."

"But how? And why?"

"I knew you had the strength within. Now is the time to use that strength."

"But I'm not strong," Senora says.

"You are stronger than you think. 'Strengthen the weak hands, and make firm the feeble knees. Say to those who have an anxious heart, 'be strong; fear not! Behold, your God will come and save you,'[94]" The man says.

"But I don't understand."

"Nora, it's time you take hold of the Greatest Treasure. You know what it is. You need to use it now. You're not alone, and He'll give you the words when the time comes," the man says to encourage her. "Don't let the darkness in. Where light is, darkness will be forced to flee."

Senora walks to the door when she hears someone unlocking it. She grabs a lamp stand and holds above her head. As the door creaks open, she sees Lucas' head. She swings, and Lucas falls to the floor. The man nods and points toward the passageway. "Go. Find the others. You're stronger together." Senora nods and runs toward the passageway. As she looks over her shoulder to thank the man, he's gone.

Soon Senora recognizes the passageway as the same one they took before to the throne room. Within seconds, Delores, Crystal, Kat, Sam, and Josiah come into view. "Nora, I thought they caught you. How did you escape?" Josiah hugs her.

---

[94]   Isaiah 35:3-4

"I had help."

"Who?" Delores asks.

"Jo, I saw the tall, bearded man again." Josiah nods with understanding.

"Who are you talking about? What tall bearded man?"

"He has appeared throughout my journey. But he's never around long enough for me to know more about him," Josiah says.

"Delores…"

"Not now, Nora, we need to focus. We're here," Delores yells.

Delores leans with her ear pressed close to listen. All is silent. The group of six slowly and quietly enter the throne room. Delores sees Scarlett sitting by the tall window. "Queen Scarlett?" she asks quietly.

Scarlett is startled out of her own thoughts. "Delores?"

"Mom?" Katarina says cautiously.

"Kat?" Kat stands cautiously at a distance.

"Lucas. He has controlled and confused you for years," Delores says.

Scarlett raises her hand to silence her. "You're the traitor, Delores, so don't try to blame anyone else but yourself," Scarlett yells.

"Queen Scarlett, you need to know something," Senora says.

"Enough." A flash of light fills the room. When everyone's eyes re-adjust, before them stands the Silver Dragon. Sam quickly stands between her and the rest.

"This is madness. I will not let you destroy another kingdom." Sam transforms into the Red Dragon.

"You? I thought I was rid of all your kind. There can only be one." The Silver Dragon flies up into the rafters of the throne room with Sam flying after her. The Silver Dragon suddenly turns and swings her tail at Sam. Sam snags her claw into the Silver Dragons tail. A loud piercing roar echoes the rafters. The Silver Dragon rams Sam hard against the wall.

Sam turns her head and bites the Silver Dragon on the neck. Scarlett screams out in pain and releases Sam from her hold. As Scarlett is distracted, Sam breaths a blast of fire towards the Silver Dragon. A loud scream is heard, and the Silver dragon falls to the floor, leaving Scarlett lying there in a weakened state.

"Mom, are you ok?" Katarina asks with tears in her eyes.

"Careful, Kat. It might not yet be safe." Sam lands on the floor with a thud and transforms back into her human form. She runs to Scarlet and props up her head.

"Sam, you were right."

"Right about what?" Sam asks.

"Lucas has been giving her an elixir. He has been trying to bring the Silver Dragon back," Senora tells them.

"Nora, how do you know this?" Delores asks.

"You were right," Scarlett says.

"Lucas told me. He also said to completely bring her back, he has to destroy the Greatest Treasure. He wants to snuff out the light for good."

Katarina walks toward Scarlett and Sam. "You were right," Scarlett says again. "Kat...."

Crystal runs to Scarlett's side and hugs her. "Mom, I love you."

"Crystal, Kat. 'Whoever speaks the truth give honest evidence, but the false witness utters deceit.[95]'" Senora says.

"Mom, I am here. We're together," Crystal says. "Friendship is a bond, but family is unbreakable."

"For where your treasure is, there your heart will be also,[96]" Senora says.

"The good person out of his good treasure brings forth good,[97]" Scarlett says.

---

[95] Proverbs 12:17
[96] Matthew 6:21
[97] Matthew 12:35a

Senora steps towards Scarlett. "If you confess with your mouth Jesus is Lord and believe in your heart that God raised him from the dead, you will be saved. For the scripture says, 'Everyone who believes in Him will not be put to shame.'[98]"

"God loves you, Scarlett. His forgiveness is great. He loves Kat and Crystal too. Please, repent, and God will save you," Josiah says, "Scarlett, what things were you finalizing?" Josiah asks.

"Lucas. He has controlled and confused me for years. I was trying to decide how to show his true loyalties. He has a strong backing."

"Yes, but all he has ordered or said he has done in your name," Senora replies. "It's you the guards follow."

"Nora, you carry the Greatest Treasure within. Stand firm. You can save us all," Scarlett says.

The throne door flies open, and Lucas enters followed by five guards. "Queen Scarlett." Lucas bows and says, "What did you do? Guards remove this monster. Goodbye, Sam. Thanks for your help."

"Help? What help?"

"You still don't know, do you?" Lucas scoffs as the guard approaches Queens Scarlett and Sam.

"Stop." Katarina yells. "I'm next in line. So, if my mom is unable to rule, I'm in charge." The guards stop and stare at Katarina expectantly.

"What are you waiting for? Arrest all of these criminals." Lucas yells.

"Criminals?" Senora asks, "We're not criminals."

Scarlett embraces her daughters. "How could you say my daughters are criminals?" Lucas looks up surprised to hear Scarlett's words.

He looks over at Senora and Josiah, and then he smiles cleverly. "No, not Crystal and Kat. But those two. They're

---

[98]   Romans 10:9b

the ones who kidnapped your daughters in the first place. I saved them."

"Liar," Katarina screams. Lucas frowns at Katarina. Scarlett holds up her hand for silence.

"Why did you deceive me, Lucas?"

"Deceive you? I love you," Lucas says.

"Do you even know what love is?" Crystal asks.

"I was talking to Queen Scarlett. Not you," Lucas abruptly responds.

"Stop right there, Lucas. Crystal is right. Do you know what true love really is?" Scarlett asks.

Lucas slowly stands to his feet. He places his hands on his hips and takes a deep breath. "Love? Love you say? Love is caring for someone and protecting them."

"Protecting them? Ok. How is making me forget my own daughters, protecting me?" Scarlett asks.

"Losing them hurt, but if you didn't have to worry about them anymore, you didn't hurt," Lucas cleverly replies.

"Taking someone you love away from them is not loving them at all," Delores says.

"Love's not that we love God but that God first loved us and gave His life for us." Senora says.

Josiah sees the tall, bearded man standing in the shadows. He taps Senora on the shoulder and points toward the man. Senora nods, and the tall, bearded man nods back at the two of them, and then vanishes. Senora turns Josiah to face her. "We need to use the Greatest Treasure. God's with us and will give us the words. Are you with me?" Senora asks.

"I am with you, Nora. All the way." The two turn to face Scarlett, Lucas, and the others.

"The Lord is my strength and my song, and he has become my salvation; this is my God, and I will praise him, my father's God, and I will exalt him.[99]"

---

[99] Exodus 15:2

"What did you say?" Lucas glares at Senora.

"Wisdom gives strength to the wise man more than ten rulers who are in a city.[100]" Josiah stands boldly beside his sister.

"Love's not that we love God, but that God first loved us and gave His life for us," Senora says.

"Strengthen the souls of the disciples; encourage them to continue in the faith, and saying that, through many tribulations, we must enter the kingdom of God.[101]" Senora feels her strength growing.

"Silence that girl," Lucas yells.

"You will do no such thing." Orders Katarina.

"For I long to see you, that I may impart to you some spiritual gifts to strengthen you,[102]" Josiah says.

"Can't you see this is mutiny? They're trying to overthrow Queen Scarlett's rule," Lucas yells at the guards.

"Now to him who is able to strengthen you according to my gospel and the preaching of Jesus Christ, according to the revelation of the mystery that was kept secret for long ages.[103]"

"You were right," she whispers again.

"For this reason, I bow my knees before the father.[104]" Senora falls to her knees. "From whom every family in heaven and on earth is named.[105]"

"Will you be silenced?" Lucas screams at Senora.

"That according to the riches of his glory he may grant you to be strengthened with power through his Spirit in your inner being.[106]"

---

[100] Ecclesiastes 7:19
[101] Acts 14:22
[102] Romans 1:11
[103] Romans 16:25
[104] Ephesians 3:14
[105] Ephesians 3:15
[106] Ephesians 3:16

Lucas runs toward Senora, but Josiah moves between them. "Get out of my way, boy."

"So that Christ may dwell in your hearts through faith which you being rooted and grounded in love, may have strength to comprehend with all the saints what is the breadth and length and height and depth.[107]" Lucas pushes Josiah to the floor and punches Senora, knocking her unconscious.

"And to know the love of Christ that surpasses knowledge, that you may be filled with all the fullness of God,[108]" Scarlett says, finishing the word. "Kat? I feel strange."

"Mom? Is that really you or another trick?" Crystal asks, concerned.

"She has had control for a long time, but when Nora used the Greatest Treasure, the darkness started to flee." Scarlett stands.

Senora starts to wake again, her head screaming in pain. Josiah helps her to her feet. "Nora, are you ok?"

"Thank you, Nora. You're bringing the light back. Thank you for not losing faith." Scarlett smiles at her.

Lucas hangs his head and sighs in frustration. He suddenly looks up and says, "If I cannot have you, then no one will." Lucas reaches behind his back, pulls out a black revolver pistol and swings his hand around pointing the gun at Scarlett.

"No," Senora screams as she runs toward Scarlett, and the guards run toward Lucas. The gun fires so loudly that Josiah's ears ring. The guards take the gun from his hands, but it appears to be too late.

"Queen Scarlett, are you safe?" one of the guards asks. Everyone looks toward the queen.

"No." Josiah screams as he sees Senora lying limp in Queen Scarlett's arms, blood on her shoulder. Josiah runs to Senora's

---

[107] Ephesians 3:17-18
[108] Ephesians 3:19

side with tears filling his eyes. He takes Senora from Scarlett's arms and turns her to face him.

Senora coughs. She reaches up her hand to touch Josiah's cheek, "Be strong and courageous. Do not be frightened and do not be discouraged for the Lord your God is with you wherever you go.[109]" Senora closes her eyes to rest as Josiah hugs his sister and cries. Senora whispers in Josiah's ear, "I understand now. The Greatest Treasure is eternal life with God. Forgiveness and belief in His sacrifice is what saves us. God does not lie. The truth will set us free. Forgive me, Jo. I have made many mistakes in my life, but please know that I love you and I admire your strength."

Josiah brushes his hand over his sister's pain-stricken face. She coughs a little and closes her eyes. "Jo, God is with us, and He has a plan. If we're together or apart, He's the one who unifies us. Our combined strength is found in His unification." Josiah sees Senora's eyes roll back into her head as she falls limp.

"No, Nora. I was supposed to protect you. Please don't go. I can't lose you too. Not like Trevor." He pulls Senora close and cries into her shoulder.

Delores walks up to Josiah and places her hand on his shoulder. "There is still hope, Jo," She says as she looks up at Scarlett.

"I don't know where it is," Scarlett says sadly.

"You'll never find it," Lucas yells.

"Guards, take him away," Scarlett says. The guards remove Lucas.

"Jo, do you remember the eagle pendant?" Delores asks.

With Josiah's eyes still closed, he slowly nods his head. *Yes* is his reply.

"Jo, reach into your pocket," Delores says softly. He removes the eagle necklace from his pocket and shows it to Delores.

---

[109] Joshua 1:9

Delores looks up at Scarlett. "You know what to do. Please help her."

"She has to want to live. I know her faith is strong but is her will?" Scarlett asks.

"We have to try." Scarlett nods and holds onto the pendant and Josiah's hand, placing both on Senora's wounded shoulder. She looks up at the sky. "Holy Father, may Your power come. They who wait for the Lord shall renew their strength; they shall mount up with wings like eagles; they shall run and not be weary; they shall walk and not faint.[110] In Jesus Name, Amen." Scarlett's golden hair starts to glow like sunshine, the light moves from her hair, down her neck, over her shoulder, and down her arm. Senora's wound starts to glow, and the light vanishes.

Senora opens her eyes, and Josiah sees that her wound is healing. He hugs her close. "Thank you, Jesus."

Senora sleepily looks up at Scarlett. "I'm glad you're safe." She smiles.

"You both helped me." Scarlett smiles in return.

Senora turns to look at Josiah. "We now understand what the Greatest Treasure is."

"She needs her rest," Delores says, "She's still quite weak." One of the guards re-enters, picks up Senora, and carries her out. "You should rest now too, Jo." Josiah nods and stands. He walks out, following his sister and the guard.

Delores and Scarlett hug. "I'm glad to have you back," Delores replies.

"Thank you for believing in me," Scarlett says.

---

[110] Isaiah 40:31

CHAPTER 15

The Greatest Treasure Revealed

The guard carries Senora to another bedroom and lays her down. "Thank you," she whispers.

"Rest now. You've been through a lot." the guard says as he leaves.

Scarlett enters Senora's room. She sits on the side of the bed next to Senora. "You're a strong young lady," Scarlett says. "I think you should have this." Scarlett places the eagle necklace around Senora's neck. "It'll remind you of what God has taught you." Senora looks at the necklace and smiles.

"Thank you," she gratefully responds.

"Thank you. You and Jo have saved us all. Never forget that friendship is a bond, but family is unbreakable. Also never give up. God is with you." Scarlett hugs Senora one more time and leaves the room. Senora looks at the necklace once again and ponders all that she has been through.

Josiah enters the room, and Senora looks up at him. "Hey, how are you feeling?" he asks as he sits beside her.

"I'm a little tired but better. Thanks for asking."

Josiah hugs Senora. "Of course. I thought I had lost you."

Senora looks behind Josiah and points. Josiah looks over his shoulder to see the tall bearded man standing in the doorway. He nods. "You did well, 'His master said to him, 'Well done, good and faithful servant. You have been over a little; I will set you over much. Enter into the joy of your master.'[111]" He smiles, turns, and starts to walk away as he vanishes from view. Josiah grabs hold of both of Senora's hands and cups his own hands around them. They close their eyes. "Thank you, Jesus," Josiah prays.

When they open their eyes again, they find themselves sitting hand in hand behind a tree with the book open beside them. Josiah can see a picture in the book of himself holding Senora's hands and praying. A caption below reads:

And he shall stand and shepherd his flock in the strength of the Lord, in the majesty of the name of the Lord his God.[112]

Senora looks around in the moonlight. Suddenly, a flashlight is shone on them. "Here! Hey, everyone. I found them Jo and Nora." A police officer runs toward them. "Are you two alright? You have been gone for almost 24 hours. Can you tell me where you have been?"

Josiah opens his mouth as he tries to think of what to tell him, when he hears his mom and dad call out their names. "Nora. Jo." Their mom runs to their side and hugs both of them. Their dad runs up, and Josiah stands, preparing himself for a lecture. His dad grabs his arm and pulls him close.

---

[111] Matthew 25:21
[112] Micah 5:4

"Jo, I thought I had lost you both. It was Trevor all over again. Where were you?"

"Dad, I don't think you would believe me if I told you." Suddenly, the police officer approaches Josiah and his dad.

"Sorry to interrupt, but I need some answers." Josiah's mind starts to race with everything him and Senora have gone through. How does someone explain all of this? If you have not experienced it, how would you believe it? Suddenly, Josiah's dad pulls his phone to his ear. He turns toward Josiah and hands the phone to him.

"What is it, Dad?"

"It's Bobbie."

Josiah takes the phone from his dad. "Bobbie? Hello?" The only thing Josiah hears on the line is crying. "Bobbie? Is that you?"

"Jo? Are you safe?" Bobbie's voice is barely above a whisper.

"Bobbie? It's me, Jo. Where are you?"

"Jo, I have caused your family enough grief."

"What are you talking about, Bobbie?" The line goes dead. Josiah's heart jumps into his throat; his surroundings start to blur. He looks at his dad and hands him the phone. His face goes ghostly white. "I'm sorry, Dad, but." He looks over at Senora, who is hugging Mom. "Nora, you up for another adventure?"

Senora pulls away from Mom's embrace, "Why do you mean?"

"I think there is another life we need to save." Josiah says.

Senora nods and runs over to Josiah's side. "I'm sorry Dad. We have to go. There's something we have to do. Just trust and believe in us."

Josiah's dad places his hand on Josiah's shoulder, "I believe in you."

They take off running toward Bobbie's house, push open the front door, and run to the basement. They stop at the bottom of the stairs, and stand there facing Bobbie. Bobbie's sitting on the floor holding a revolver in his hands. "Bobbie, you don't need to do this." Josiah says.

"What do you know about it? I only cause grief and hardship. I destroyed your family and mine."

"No, you didn't. It was not your fault." Senora says.

"Not my fault? You weren't there that night. I was the one who pulled the trigger. I killed Trevor."

"It was not your fault. Trevor tried to save you. He died so you could live. Bobbie, there's a reason you're here. Don't throw it all away like this." Senora says.

"What do you know about it? I ruin everything I touch." Robert says.

"That's a lie. You're loved more than anything. What would your death do to your mom? To me? To Nora? We all make mistakes, but we're stronger when we choose to learn from our mistake and move forward. Trevor wouldn't want you to die. If you pull that trigger, it's as if you're saying that Trevor's death meant nothing." Josiah says.

"Trevor was my best friend. His life meant everything to me." Robert says.

"Then don't make his death meaningless. Your life matters. Friendship is a bond and family is unbreakable. You have friendship with us, and your mom would never be the same if you were gone." Senora says.

"Everyone would be better off without me." Robert says.

"I used to think that about myself too. Death seemed like to only comfort or answer after Trevor died. For I know the plans I have for you, declares the Lord, plans to prosper you and not to harm you, plans to give you hope and a future.[113]" Senora says.

"Plan? Nora, there are no plans for me. Only destruction. I have no future."

---

[113] Jeremiah 29:11

"You are stronger than this, Bobbie. Do not allow the lies to take hold. You have a purpose and a life." Senora says.

"What kind of life do I have?" Robert says.

"You have a choice to live or die. But the pain you leave behind will only cause the destruction to grow." Senora says.

"The thief comes only to steal and to kill and destroy; I have come that they may have life, and have it to the full.[114]" Josiah says.

"Life to its fullest? I have no life. I only make everyone else miserable." Robert says.

"Listen to me, Bobbie. I know life seems pretty dark right now but trust me it will only get darker if you take your life. Cast your burdens on the Lord, and He will sustain you; He will never permit the righteous be moved.[115]" Senora says.

"My whole world is shaken. My dad hates me; my mom is too scared to leave the house. You only tolerate me. I have nobody." Robert says.

"Bobbie, we're here right now for you. We believe in you. Trevor believed in you. Please know that you have a purpose, and your life does matter. Please, Bobbie, don't lose hope. Therefore, there is no condemnation for those who are in Christ Jesus, because through Christ Jesus the law of the spirit who gives life has set you free from the law of sin and death.[116]" Josiah says.

"That's just it, Jo. Death is the only release from this pain." Robert says.

"No, Bobbie. The pain will only grow. You're one of the strongest people I know. You're not a coward. Don't take the coward's way out. Prove to yourself that you're strong enough to survive and learn." Senora says.

---

[114] John 10:10
[115] Psalm 55:22
[116] Romans 8:1-2

"Learn? What is there to learn? Life's just full of misery and disappointment." Robert says.

"I know it looks like that right now, but I'm here, and I'm not willing to give up on you. Please don't give up on yourself." Josiah takes a few more steps closer to Bobbie as the gun loosens in Bobbie's grip. "For I am confident that neither death nor life, neither angel nor demon, neither the present nor the future, nor any powers, neither height nor depth, nor anything else in all creation, will be able to separate us from the love of God that is in Christ Jesus, our Lord.[117]" Josiah says.

Josiah reaches out his hand as the gun falls from Bobbie's fingers. He quickly takes the gun and locks it in the gun safe. Senora runs to Bobbie's side and hugs him. "I'm sorry. With Trevor, with everything." Robert says.

"Bobbie, I forgive you. Now, let's move forward together. There's a God in heaven who wants to know you personally. He has loved you even when you hated him. Now that you're His child why would He stop loving you?" Josiah says as he walks back to Robert and Senora's side.

"I'm sorry; I don't know what else to do." Robert says.

"Live as an adopted child of God. He will never leave you. You're never alone. I believe in you, and I'm here for you anytime." Senora says as Bobbie cries into his knees.

As Senora and Josiah return, they see their parents arguing. "Where's did they go? Did you lose them again?" Mom says.

"Their fine. They went to talk to Bobbie."

"What? You let them go talk to Bobbie? Are you crazy? Do you want to lose them like you lost Trevor? Nora and Jo

---

[117] Romans 8:38-39

have been missing for almost 24 hours and you let him go again? How could you?"

"Look, Jo said it was important."

"That's what you say. How could you let them go?"

"Mom, stop." Senora takes her mom's hand.

"I knew it was a mistake to come home. Even if you two were missing."

Their dad turns to walk away. "Dad, wait." Josiah runs to his dad. "Dad, I love you, and as you can see, Nora and I are fine. But you need to stop running." Josiah says.

"Running? What am I running from? You know I have to work." Dad says.

"Yes, but Trevor wouldn't want you to push us away. We need you now more than ever." Josiah takes his dad's hand and walks him back toward Mom. He reaches out and grabs Mom's hand with his free hand. "Mom, we're stronger together. I know we're all hurting. We all miss Trevor. But Trevor would not want us to stop believing in each other. We need to be strong when the other is weak." He places her mom's hand in Dad's hand. "Only together can we move forward. 'For this reason I bow my knees before the Father, from whom every family in heaven and on earth is named, that according to the riches of his glory he may grant you to be strengthened with the power through his Spirit in your inner being, so that Christ may dwell in your hearts through faith-that you, being rooted and grounded in love, may have strength to comprehend with all the saints what is the breadth and length and height and depth, and to know the love of Christ that surpasses knowledge, that you may be filled with all the fullness of God.[118]" Senora says cupping her hands around Josiah's, and her parents hands.

---

[118] Ephesians 3:14-19

Dad looks from his hand up into his wife's tear filled eyes. He pulls her close into a hug. "I'm sorry; I forgot you were hurting too." Dad says.

"I just miss him so much, and when Nora and Jo went missing, I just didn't know what to do." Mom says.

"I understand. It would have destroyed both of us if we had lost them too." Dad says.

"Mom, Dad, family is unbreakable. We're strongest when we stand together." Josiah says.

"How did you get so smart?" his dad asks.

They both smile and Senora unconsciously twirls her fingers around the chain that she wears around her neck. She looks at the eagle pendant that dangles freely from the chain. "You know, I would like to know where you were all this time and where you got that necklace from. It seems to have just appeared," her mom says.

Senora allows the chain to fall from her fingers, looks up at her parents and simply smiles. "Maybe someday, but now is not the time. Friendship is a bond, but family is unbreakable."

Scripture Index

Footnotes

Author Bio

Lorie Gurnett is a Soul of Fire. Through her writing, speaking, and singing, she encourages others to overcome fear in their lives, discover how much God loves them, the importance of unity within both the family of God and individual families, and encourages others to use their strength to pursue their dreams.

Lorie struggled to understand her true identity in Christ. As a young lady, she suffered with suicidal thoughts, emotions of being invisible, and that she had nothing important to say. Today, Lorie understands that she is God's child and even when she hated God, He still loved her. Now that she is his child, why would He stop loving her? Lorie has been happily married for 19 years and has 2 teenage children, who are such a blessing to her. She is determined to reach those who are hurting and be God's arms of love. Everyone is important and deserving of love and forgiveness.

You've read the book

Are you ready to discover your true identity?

You can go on a journey of self discover.

Explore what God says about you.

Rise to your True potential.

Treasure Kingdom Discovery

**Gateway to discovering your Identity and
Rise to your Full Potential**

Go on a 40 day experience of self discovery, hope, healing,
and forgiveness.

www.treasurekingdom.com

FEAR

Fear Breaker
Breaking the Bondage of Fear
6 day series.

Do you desire to overcome fear in your life?

Get you Content here:
www.treasurekingdom.com

CPSIA information can be obtained
at www.ICGtesting.com
Printed in the USA
FFHW022003031019
55348500-61089FF

9 781640 856707